Shaded Grove

Oliver C. Seneca

Stag
Beetle
Books

For my team: Kelmich Agosto, Ashley Rosado, Damien Holmes, Natalie Miller, Autumn Marou, Karla and Jessica Dumas, Missy Brenneman, Tiffany Golobek, Vikki Williams, and Becki Hatzimichael.

Thank you for saving my life.

Contents

Chapter 1

The Old Woman

Megan Willis kept her hands at ten and two on the steering wheel of the Ford as raindrops splattered the windshield. The wipers slashed furiously at the droplets.

"Great," she said with her eyes trained on the road. The windshield wipers went full speed, swiping away at the endless drops. "This is *just* great. You just had to find a stupid ghost tour all the way out here in the middle of nowhere."

Dianne sat in the passenger seat with her knees tucked against her chest. She swiped at her phone almost in sync with the violent wipers.

"Unbelievable," Megan said to herself before she shook a strand of black hair from her eyes. "Are you watching the GPS? If I miss the turn, we're screwed. It's so dangerous out here. I have no idea where we are."

"I'm watching it," Dianne replied, glancing up at Megan's phone that sat in a holder wedged into the vent on the dash. "We still have a mile and a half before turning left on Grove Street."

Soaked, dead trees lined either side of the foreign back-road. A pickup truck in the oncoming lane whizzed by with its high beams on, making Megan scream out, "Slow down!" Then to Dianne, "The people out here are driving like maniacs!"

"Just relax, Meg. It's all right. We're gonna be ok," Dianne said.

"You're not the one who has to drive in this mess," Megan replied. "God, I mean, this is just stupid. Driving out here to hear a stupid ghost story and tour a smelly house, just so we can take some pictures and drive home in the rain. How can you believe in this stuff? Honestly..."

Dianne didn't take the bait. Instead, she just sat in a frustrated silence until the robot woman's voice played from the phone on the vent, informing the sisters to turn left onto Grove Street.

Once she was sure no other cars would come careening around the corner, Megan slowed the Ford, easing it across the wet intersection. "All right, how much longer now?"

"Looks like nine miles until the turnpike ramp is on our right," Dianne replied.

"Great, let's get out of this backwoods town," Megan said.

The rain did not relent.

"For your birthday next year, pick a haunted house closer to home. Or, better yet, no haunted house at all! Just be a normal person and ask for an Amazon gift card or something."

Dianne sighed and said, "Listen, I appreciate you taking me. I'm sorry about the weather and all this. It won't happen again, all right?" Her tone became sincere. "I'll *never* bother you again."

"Maybe if you got yourself a boyfriend who was into

this stuff, the two of you could travel all over the country, seeing all kinds of spooky places," Megan said. "Just think of all the wonderful adventures you could have. You could talk to all the ghosts you'd like!"

"All right. Stop. I get it."

But Megan didn't stop. She kept up the aggression, chipping away at Dianne's patience.

Like all siblings across the globe, Megan always knew how to get under Dianne's skin with an extra comment, another jab. As much as Dianne wanted to be the bigger person and let her older sister's words roll off her back, everyone had a tipping point.

So, as the car crept down the soaked asphalt, the sisters began a back and forth, throwing insults at one another, their voices growing louder with every criticism.

Dianne turned back to her phone. *Let it roll off your back,* she thought to herself. Instead, the insult rolled off her tongue. "Megan, *you're* the one who's always pissed off and —with your inability to have fun, you kill every party you've been invited to!"

It came out more like a scream than she'd intended.

"Oh yeah? Well, you're a spoiled brat who is too stupid to do *anything* for yourself. That's why I'm the one stuck driving you home from some *stupid* haunted house," Megan fired back, raised voice matching that of her sister's. "It makes sense, though; only braindead morons would believe in ghosts, tarot cards, and psychics."

The sister-on-sister brutality went on for almost two full miles until Megan slammed her foot on the brake pedal, making the Ford slide to the left, then right, then back to the left again. Megan's phone flew from the holder on the vent, while Dianne's dropped from between her fingers. An empty Starbucks cup bounced out from beneath the backseats. Loose change shot out from the cupholders like metal confetti.

Megan screamed as she tried to regain control of the wheel.

Dianne shouted in fright as the headlights spun with the vehicle, reflecting off the rainfall and illuminating an old woman standing near the double yellow lines on the road in a flash.

The car slid onto the grassy patch next to the road, stopping just before the trees. Everything fell suddenly still and silent, with only the sound of the pouring rain pounding the car.

Megan and Dianne stared at each other for a moment, breathing in gasps as Megan had the brake pedal pushed down so hard that it touched the carpeted mat beneath it. She threw the gear into park.

"Oh, my God," Megan whispered, her face painted in a panicked white. "Are you all right?"

Dianne nodded. Black strands of her hair went every which way.

"Did we...?" She swallowed, a heavy lump in her throat. Her heart hammered against her chest. Nausea took over. "Did we hit that lady?"

Without hesitation, Megan took off her seatbelt and kicked the driver-side door open to find the old woman approaching the car. Dianne followed, drenched clothes be damned.

A short woman in a soaked long-sleeved sweater swayed in the dark. She was frail, her slippers and hair drenched.

"Ma'am, I am so sorry! I didn't see you in the road," Megan said as she moved closer to the old woman, extending her arms as if to hug her. Rain pelted her leather jacket. "Are you okay? Are you hurt?"

The old woman nodded and said, "Oh, yes. I'm just fine. I'm terribly sorry I got in your way. I really didn't mean to. Please forgive me."

Dianne came around the Ford and opened the door to the backseat. "Let's get her out of this rain."

With quickened steps, and one hand pressed on a bony back, Megan led the old woman to the open door and helped her sit down. Once safe inside, Megan shut the door and climbed into the driver seat as Dianne sat beside the old woman in the back, eyeing her up and down beneath the tiny dome light, checking for any injury.

Her short, gray hair dripped onto the faded sweater she wore. Wrinkles and liver spots covered her skin, and her hands shook with a slight tremor. No blood. No cuts. Not even a bruise. The lady didn't even seem panicked. Although Megan and Dianne breathed heavily, scared out of their minds, the old woman sat facing forward without a care in the world, smiling with grayed teeth like she just got away with something.

"Why were you out in the street with it raining like this?" Megan asked between breaths. She knelt on the front seat, leaning toward the old woman and her sister in the back, trying to see her condition for herself.

"Oh, well...." The old woman blinked. She thought for a moment. "You know, I can't say for certain. I know I was tidying up my room." A slight chuckle came from her. "Next thing I know, I'm outside in the pouring rain. When you get to be my age, your mind gets a little fuzzy." She looked over at Dianne with her brown eyes unblinking. "You're a very pretty, young girl. You won't have to worry about forgetting things for a long time."

Dianne gave a slight smile. "Thank you, but maybe we should get you to a hospital."

"Oh, no, no. Really, I don't want any trouble," the old woman said, touching Dianne's leg with a shaking, wet hand. "Just back to my room is fine. I'd hate to get in your way, especially in this weather. I wouldn't want either of you to catch something."

Dianne exchanged a glance with Megan, who met her gaze, but was somehow keeping her expression calm.

"Do you live around here?" Megan asked as she started to search for her phone among the thrown trash inside the car. "Is there a family member I can call? We're more worried about *you* getting sick. We wanna make sure you're all right."

The old woman paused again. Her eyes moved toward Megan. "Family? A family member? Like a daughter or grandchild?"

"Yes," Dianne said. "Is there someone we can contact to let them know we have you? That you're safe?"

The old woman turned her head back to face Dianne. Her eyebrows moved around, slightly curling.

"What's your name?" Megan asked as she picked up her phone from the side of her seat. "Or your address?"

The old woman's face contorted in response. Her lips trembled. Her cheeks twitched.

"Ma'am, are you all right?" Dianne asked, leaning close. The woman didn't respond. Instead her eyes fluttered. Terror struck Dianne as she believed the old woman was having a stroke or some type of seizure. "Ma'am?" She looked over at her sister with panicked eyes. "Meg...."

"Can you hear us?" Megan asked, getting the same response her sister did. "Oh, Jesus." With shaking hands, she scrambled to unlock her phone and dial 911. Before the call could be initiated, the old woman began to shout and shake, pushing Dianne away.

"*No! I do not want you to call the authorities! You cannot do that to me! Not again!*" Her harsh voice sliced through the damp air inside the car. She shot forward, trying to grab Megan's phone, but Megan clung it against her chest. "Just take me back to my room if you must! But that's all!"

The sisters stared at each other for a moment, unable to speak or move.

"Ok," Megan said, trying to ease the situation. "All right. No problem. But you'll have to help us. Where exactly is your room? Where do you live?"

The old woman's face hung low, disappointed. "Oh, you don't know?"

"No, ma'am," Megan said. "Perhaps you could tell us so we can take you there." She lowered her phone out of the woman's view, muted the sound, and typed *HOSPITALS NEAR ME* in the search bar of the GPS app. An uncomfortably long moment passed before the results popped up. Megan pressed on the first option, bringing up the route to Golden Creek Medical Center. Twenty-six miles away; seeing that distance was almost as frustrating as the fact that she couldn't express her stress from seeing it. "How about a phone number? Do you live with your family?"

The old woman folded her arms and looked away, facing the ceiling. Her mood changed by the second, like any word could send her into a different attitude.

"Ma'am?" Megan said.

The old woman's eyes shifted back and forth. A slight groan came from her throat.

Megan pushed the shift into drive. She drove with one hand on the wheel while holding her phone in the other, keeping it by her thigh.

"Everything's going to be all right," Dianne said softly to

the old woman as the Ford kicked up mud and grass, shooting back onto the road.

The rain continued to pour, and Megan had to keep the windshield wipers on full power as she started to speed up the darkened backroad, hoping the old woman wouldn't die or throw a fit before she made it to the emergency room. She cranked the heat up with the knob on the dashboard so that pneumonia wouldn't set in either.

"Hold onto her, strap her in," Megan said. "I'm going as fast as I can."

Dianne did so, never taking her eyes off the old woman. "Just be careful, Meg." She put on her seatbelt and did the same for the old woman. It took a second to maneuver around her body, but she clicked the metal piece into the plastic, red-buttoned holster.

"We're going back to your room, okay?" Megan said, clicking on her seatbelt as well. "Just sit tight."

More groans came from the woman. Her eyes darted until she lowered her head and met Dianne's eyes again. Under the dome light, the sockets of her eyes became hollow, like dark spots staring into Dianne's soul.

"You know," the old woman said. "You really are a pretty girl."

Dianne gave a slight nod and a half-hearted smile, masking her discomfort.

"You're the spitting image of your mother." That bizarre smile returned to the old woman's face, more grayed than before. "You have her eyes and that dark black hair." Her shaky hands touched Dianne's dripping hair and caressed it between her scaly fingers before moving down to touch her cheeks.

Megan tried to watch the road and her sister in the

rearview mirror at the same time. Her eyes widened at the sight of the old lady's touch.

"Tell me. Has she been telling lies about me?" the old woman asked Dianne. "Nasty things?" Her breath stunk with a musty stench.

"I...." Dianne didn't have the slightest clue on how to respond. "I don't know what you're talking about."

"Your mother!" the old woman shouted. It made Megan jerk the wheel slightly, sending the old woman onto Dianne. Dianne carefully pushed the woman away as Megan steered the Ford back into the lane.

"Sorry!" Megan said. "Please, ma'am. Just calm down."

The old woman turned from Dianne. "Calm down? Let me guess, you're brainwashed, too!"

Megan shot her eyes up to the mirror again but had to return her focus to the slick and shiny road. "Ma'am...."

"Lies, lies! All they tell you are lies!" The old woman reached up and grabbed Megan's arm with a surprising grip. Megan didn't fight back as she kept control of the wheel. "They're making me out to be the devil. The devil!" She squeezed tighter, making Megan shift her arm. The movement made her phone fall from her thigh, landing somewhere she couldn't see. "How could you believe them when you don't even know me!?"

Dianne grabbed the old woman's arm, but the woman's rage grew. "You have no right to touch me!" Her body jerked to the side. An audible clicking noise came, but it wasn't her bones. It was the seatbelt coming out of the holster.

"Don't!" Dianne said, reaching for the old woman, who jumped up into the front of the Ford. "Stop!"

The car swerved as Megan began to shout and throw her arms in the air, trying to keep the manic woman at bay.

Dianne grabbed the old woman's feet but instead got her slippers as the soaked, fluffy things slid right off her socks.

The old woman began to mash her fists against Megan, making the car swerve hard into the grass again. The headlights whipped, shooting across the night until Megan straightened the wheel. She tried to press down on the brake pedal but got hit again by the crazed woman.

"Lies! Lies!" the old woman shouted.

"Hey!" Dianne screamed. Just before she unhooked her seatbelt and yanked the old woman away from her sister, the Ford jerked hard to the left, flying off the road before it started to descend the wooded hill beside the road.

Dead trees blurred past the windows. The car bounced and slid fast down the embankment until it met a tree stump, causing the Ford to roll onto its side, flipping again and again.

The old woman shrieked as her body got shoved hard above the dashboard, smashing against the windshield.

The two sisters closed their eyes.

Chapter 2

Shaded Grove Mental Hospital

Dianne woke up first. Her vision blurred, showing her a dim, flickering glow of the broken dome light below. Her arms ached as she brought them up to rub her eyes, and a deep pain pulsed within her skull. It took Dianne a few seconds to blink and bring a bit of focus to her surroundings.

Garbage and glass littered around the cracked plastic of the dome light, which flashed a slight orange light in brief bursts. Up front, Megan's body dangled in silence before the cobweb-shattered windshield, her hair a wild mop on her head. Dianne couldn't see any sign of the old woman.

"Megan...?" Dianne groaned. No response came.

The seatbelt held Dianne as she sat upside down in the overturned Ford. Her black hair hung like a curtain. She felt like every ounce of blood sat on the top of her head, the tip of her fingers, about to pop. Even her feet slightly dangled, feeling weighted, like the blood rushed into her sneakers, making them swell up like balloons.

With slow hands, Dianne reached behind her to feel for the seat belt holster. Once her fingers found the plastic button, she angled her legs as best as she could to stop the inevitable drop. She also placed her other arm behind the headrest, holding the cushion with as much strength as she could muster. But before she clicked free, Dianne heard her sister start to stir. A slight relief came over her.

"Mmm. What? What...what the...?" Megan whispered. "Di-Dianne?"

"I'm here," Dianne replied, her throat bone-dry. "Are you all right?"

Megan examined her arms, then down at her inverted body. "I have no idea. I can barely see in here. My head is killing me. Are you okay?"

"I'm shaken up, but I don't think I broke anything," Dianne said. "Not sure if I'm bleeding anywhere, though."

"That old lady...that crazy woman...."

"I know, but we have to get out of here. I'm gonna come down and unhook you."

"Are you sure that's a good idea?"

"What else am I supposed to do?"

"I don't know. Call 911?" Megan coughed. Her voice shook. "Hey, Siri."

Megan's phone didn't respond, didn't make a sound.

"Hey, Siri." She struggled to speak louder.

Still nothing.

Dianne tried calling out to her own phone's virtual assistant, but no reply came from anywhere in the smashed car.

"Great," Megan sighed. "And this thing doesn't have Onstar." She turned her body, trying to get a look below for her phone.

"Just relax," Dianne said, not sounding too calm herself. "I'm coming to get you."

Dianne unlocked her seat belt and carefully lowered

herself down from the hanging back seat, but not without a few jolts of pain that shocked her bones. She felt like a ragdoll.

"Watch the glass," Megan said.

"I know." Dianne crouched and crawled between the headrests of the front seats. "Can you grab the back of the seat and hold yourself up for a second? I'm gonna unstrap you, but you have to go slow and steady."

Megan cursed some more but got leverage with her arm and the headrest as Dianne took her seat belt off. Everything was so crammed and tight.

"Easy now," Dianne said.

Megan winced and lowered herself down beside her sister as the two of them crawled close together on the turned roof of the Ford.

"Your head," Megan said, eyeing her younger sister. "You have a little cut by your right eye. It doesn't look too bad, though."

Dianne touched the spot, feeling wetness near her temple. A small trickle of blood spilled halfway down her cheek. "Thanks. I can't see any blood on you from what I can tell."

"What about our phones?"

"I didn't see them," Dianne said. "What if they flew out of the car?"

The sisters fell silent for a second.

"All right, c'mon," Megan said, looking at all the shards of glass and trash that surrounded them. She noticed the broken window by the driver's seat. "I'm gonna break us out. Close your eyes for a sec."

Angling herself like a crab, Megan got as low as she could make herself on the roof of the Ford, currently serving as the floor, being careful not to slice her hands with the glass that peppered all around her. She leaned back and began to kick the window with her heavy black boot, breaking away chunks of glass with every hit.

"Let me go first," she said.

Dianne watched her sister crawl through the barely big enough hole in the window and step out into the dark.

"Well, there goes this shirt," Megan said from outside. "Ripped right down the middle. Hold on, don't go yet." She hooked her boot into the window and chipped away some of the remaining bits of glass. She took off her leather jacket and laid it over the opening. "All right. Go very slowly, and make sure you suck your stomach in as much as you can."

Being thin like her sister, Dianne escaped the over-turned Ford with ease. No shards of sharp glass tore through her shirt or jacket as she made it out to meet Megan beneath the drizzling night sky.

The sisters embraced, each with tears starting to blur their vision, but they couldn't waste another moment.

"At least the rain let up," Dianne said, taking in the surroundings of the black trees, surprised that the car landed in a clearing and not tangled among the dead bark.

"Where do you think that lady is?" Megan asked.

"She's probably dead, Meg. Somewhere out here in the woods. She didn't have her seatbelt on," Dianne answered as another wave of nausea came over her. "*We're* lucky to be alive."

Megan didn't say anything as she tried to let her eyes adjust to the dark. She turned and knelt by the Ford, looking from the outside to see if their phones were anywhere inside. The chill of the night swept through the girls.

"What are we gonna do now?" Dianne asked.

"We have to get back to the road. Any idea which direction that's in?"

"What about the woman?"

"Once we get back to the road, we can worry about her. For right now, we need to get help. There's no sense trying to find her when we can't see anything."

"Right...." Dianne sighed.

One could only imagine the questions they'd have to answer once they found help. What were they doing all the way out here? *Well, officer, we did a ghost house tour, it's kind of a tradition*—How did they almost hit the elderly woman? That question would be harder, considering she seemed to both appear and vanish in the blink of an eye. Lastly—most importantly—the "help" they found would no doubt remind the sisters how lucky they were to be alive after crawling out of their destroyed Ford.

"What's that over there?" Megan asked as her shadow moved away from Dianne and the car.

"What?" Dianne said, trying to see.

"Over there, the light. See it? Between the trees. Twelve o'clock." Megan grabbed her sister's hand and raised it, pointing it in the right direction.

Between the mangled, twisted branches of the trees, a faint—at first—orange glow could be glimpsed; it stood out in the abyss of darkness.

Dianne had to squint her eyes hard to make it out. "Yeah, I see it now."

"Maybe it's a light from a gas station or something. Maybe a house. If we find someone, we can call the police and tell them what happened. Call Mom to let her know we're fine."

"Do you know what time it is?"

"Your guess is as good as mine," Megan said. "C'mon, let's head that way. Can you walk okay?"

"Yeah, I'm good. Are you able to?"

"I have no choice," Megan replied, taking her sister's hand as she began to walk toward the distant glow. She guided Dianne the best she could, making sure to feel for any upturned roots or fallen trees. "Just tell me if you get tired and need to stop or if you're in too much pain."

Torn and frightened, the sisters walked through the black, wet wilderness with panicked steps and hammering hearts. Neither of them said much as they maneuvered through the dark, hoping to find a miracle beneath the light ahead, anything to get them out of the chaos that fell upon them as quick as the hard rain from before.

The orange light came closer and closer until the density of the trees started to dwindle. The foliage shortened and began to spread apart as the sisters stepped out of the woods and stood before a parking lot with a lone van sitting in the shadowed corner. The orange glow came from a looming light pole that towered over a chain-link fence and large metal gate. Beyond them stood brick buildings with tiny windows dotting the sides. Blackness shrouded the world beyond the streetlamp.

"What is this place?" Megan asked as she walked onto the rough asphalt of the parking lot. Tall weeds sprouted between the cracks.

"Looks abandoned to me," Dianne said. She moved toward the van, trying to see if anyone sat inside, but the rainy darkness obscured her vision.

"Look, there's a sign by the pole," Megan said, grabbing Dianne's hand again. "C'mon."

The sisters approached the opposite end of the parking lot, where the light shone down on a wooden and concrete sign with chipped painted lettering that sat before the metal gate. Beside it sat a small toll-booth structure covered in cobwebs.

"Shaded Grove Mental Hospital," Dianne said.

"Great, exactly what we were looking for!" Megan groaned. "I mean, really, could we have found a more awful place to end up at a time like this?" She moved up to the metal gate, peering between the rusty bars at the dark grounds beyond. "Hello?" Her voice grew louder. "Is anyone here? We need some help!" Megan grabbed the bars and tried to rattle the gate but had to stop immediately as a fresh wave of pain washed over her right arm. She winced as she felt the bones shift unnaturally beneath her skin. Behind gritted teeth, she shouted again. "Anyone here?"

"C'mon, Meg, let's just go. This parking lot has to connect back to the road somehow," Dianne said as she touched her sister's shoulder. "I don't like this place."

"Yeah, me neither," Megan said, turning away from the rusted bars. "But what the hell? We can't just keep wandering around out here."

The orange light illuminated the sisters' pale, filthy bodies. Between the rain and the car crash, their hairdos were all over the place. Megan had a cut straight down the middle of her gray shirt. Her leather jacket had marks on the sleeves from laying it down over the glass. Meanwhile, Dianne had a stream of blood dried against her face. Her soaked jacket weighed heavy from the rain.

"I know, but there's no one here. There's no sense in staying," Dianne said. "We can't be far from someplace else."

Megan limped alongside her sister as the two of them moved across the lonesome, pothole-riddled parking lot.

Suddenly, a voice came from behind them, making the sisters jump.

"Excuse me, ladies," a man's voice said. "What are you two doing out here?"

Megan and Dianne jolted around to see a shadow of a man standing beyond the rusted gate, shining a flashlight on them.

"Oh, thank God," Megan said under her breath as she practically ran to the bars. Dianne kept close behind. "We've been in an accident. My sister and I were almost killed! Our car is flipped in the woods, and there's a crazy old woman missing!"

"Now, just calm down a moment, please," the man said. His flashlight shined on the girls' faces, making them squint. "My goodness, you're bleeding on the side of your head, young lady. Let me open the gate so I can patch you up. Stay right there, you two. Don't go anywhere."

The man moved to the side and entered the tiny post beside the gate. Megan and Dianne saw him through the small, square-shaped window as he took out a set of keys and jammed one of them down before a faint buzzing noise sounded. The metal gate rumbled and began to open inwards.

"Ok, come on through. I'll close it behind you," the man said. The sisters wasted no time walking inside.

"Thank you," Megan said. "Do you have a phone we could use?"

The gate buzzed again before the doors swung close.

"Certainly," the man said as he exited the booth. "There's one in the Administration Building. A first-aid kit, too. Follow me."

Concrete paths created a maze in between patches of overgrown grass that led across the darkened hospital grounds. Extinguished light poles stood high above. The towering brick buildings that surrounded everything were blacked-out, the windows only reflecting the light of the moon and the light coming from the man's flashlight as he guided the girls toward the small building in the center of the walkways.

Despite the eeriness of the place's atmosphere, the sisters sighed in relief to have found another human being.

"So, tell me exactly what happened to you two. You said you were in a car accident? Are you all right?" the man asked.

"Yes," the sisters said at the same time.

"We were driving back home when this old woman was walking in the middle of the road," Megan said, trying not to get too animated with the story. She went on to explain the bizarre situation. Almost running the woman over. Trying to call 911. Her outbursts. Her shifting mood. The violent behavior that led to the car accident. How the woman was now missing. And, to finish it off, how the sisters escaped the flipped car and found the mental hospital through the woods.

The man's tone became more serious as he led Megan and Dianne into the Administration Building. "And you never saw this woman before in your lives?"

"No," Dianne said. "That's why her bringing our mom up was so creepy."

When the three of them entered the building, and the man flicked the light switch by the door, Megan and Dianne saw the man was thin and tall, wore a soaked tan uniform which included a police-ish looking hat that sat atop his buzzed hair. A patched nametag on the left side of his chest read: TODD.

"Phone's on the counter there. Go ahead and call for the

police while I fetch some bandages for you," Todd said before crossing the lobby and disappearing into a room on the other end.

The musty place had a vintage 1950s look to it. Wooden chairs lined up against the windows and a check-in desk with a fine layer of dust covering the top of it. A light-pink rotary phone sat on the check-in counter, something both Megan and Dianne hadn't seen in a very long time.

"Wow," Megan said under her breath as she approached the phone. "Hope this still works." She pulled the heavy piece of ancient technology toward the edge of the counter before placing her finger in the hole labeled 9. She spun the dial around until it clicked back. Next, she touched the 1 spot. This time, as the dial was turned, the dingy fluorescents overhead went out, shrouding the small room in pitch black. "Hey! What in the..." Megan attempted to spin the dial again, but no sound came from the speaker on the receiver. She slammed the phone down hard on the wood. "Nothing! Unbelievable...."

Todd rushed back into the room, clutching a small metal box in one hand and his flashlight in the other. "Shoot, the power must've gone out. And the phone lines, too. Maybe a car crashed into one of the poles." He approached the girls and planted the first aid kit on the counter. "Don't worry, the generators should kick on in a second."

Both sisters stood impatiently in the dark, waiting.

"Sometimes, it just takes a moment to get into gear," Todd said.

"Don't you have a cell phone?" Megan asked, but before Todd answered, the lights flickered on overhead. Megan wasted no time spinning the numbers on the dial again, however, her second chance at calling the authorities failed faster than the first attempt as the room went black again. A loud, quick popping sound came from beyond the walls.

"Oh, no," Dianne said to herself. "What was that?"

"Darn it. Listen, ladies, I'm sorry," Todd said. "There must've been a malfunction in the main generator outside. The thing has a tendency to act up every now and again." He moved past the sisters before stopping at the front door. "I need you two to just have a seat for me, get yourselves patched up as best you can with the first aid kit there. I promise this won't take long."

"Are you kidding me?" Megan said. Her voice shook with frightened anger. "You're not leaving us in here. We're coming with you."

Todd waved his flashlight around. "It will be better if you're inside. You'll be close to the phone when I get the power going again. Safer, too."

The sisters looked at each other, uncertainty painting their wide eyes.

"This will only take me a minute," Todd went on. "I'm sorry. I'll try to radio to the other guys, but until then, I have to take care of this myself." He opened the door, bringing in the chill of the night. The rain picked up again. "Before you know it, we'll have the police and an ambulance here. A search party for that woman, too. Don't worry."

Megan threw her hands in the air and started to shout, but Todd had already shut the door to the Administration Building, leaving the sisters alone in the dark. Megan went to the door to follow the security guard when Dianne grabbed her arm, sending a little jolt of pain up her elbow.

"My arm!" Megan said behind gritted teeth. "Don't touch me there!"

"Sorry," Dianne said, pulling her hand away. "But he's right. As soon as the power comes back on, we can make the call." An ominous feeling swirled in her gut. Todd. Shaded Grove Mental Hospital.

"Fine," Megan said before trying to open the metal first aid box on the counter with frantic fingers. She slid it around, feeling for the unlocking clasp with no luck. "I can't see anything in here. How do you open this?"

Dianne moved toward the room where Todd had found the first aid kit, walking slowly to not trip on anything.

"Where are you going?" Megan asked. "You just said—"

"I'm looking for a light. Calm down," Dianne replied. "There might be a flashlight or something in here."

Through the door, Dianne found herself in a tiny closet with wooden shelves on either side with various office supplies. Staplers. Binders. A glass jar of pens. Cobwebs clung to the corners. A thick sheen of dust coated everything, tickling Dianne's nose. She could just see with the slight light from the moon that shined through the little window on the top of the wall. The raindrops made tiny shadows.

Searching with squinted eyes, Dianne got down on her knees, finding documents in paper files scattered. Cardboard boxes lie smashed and thrown beneath the shelves. She moved them around, hoping to find anything to use as a light source, but instead found a family of dead rats staring back at her with skeletonized eyes, each frozen with bodies of half-bone and half-fur.

Dianne screamed and jumped up from the dusty floor, almost slamming her head against the edge of the shelf above her.

"Dianne?" Megan shouted before running to the closet herself to see her sister against the wall. "Dianne, what happened?"

Breathing heavy, Dianne replied, "Rats. Dead rats under those boxes."

Unimpressed, Megan grabbed her sister and yanked her out of the closet. "C'mon, I got the first aid kit open. Let's put a Band-Aid on your head before you break it open again."

Back in the waiting area, Megan sat Dianne down in one of the creaky chairs as she tore open a bandage from the kit, using her long nails to peel back the brittle paper that covered the adhesive strip.

"Hold still," Megan said. "I can barely see."

Dianne sat facing the window as her sister placed a Band-Aid over the cut on her right temple. A slight sting tingled through her head, but it wasn't deep. If her whole head had smashed against the window of the Ford, the night would be a lot different than it was now.

Lightning flashed outside the window, illuminating Dianne's pale, blood-streaked face for a moment. Faint thunder followed as the rain grew stronger, pattering on the roof as the moments passed, longer and longer until something caught Dianne's eye.

"I think Todd's coming back," she said as she saw a dark figure walking by outside.

Megan got up and stood by the door, waiting for the security guard to return with more bad news, to tell them that he couldn't get the generator back on. They waited for a moment. Then another. Todd didn't come back.

Lightning flashed again, showing Dianne a face through the window in front of her. Her heart began to hammer violently inside her chest. It stared at her from the bottom of the glass, like a child's head spying on her or someone hunkered down to peek into the building. She could hardly catch a breath.

"Meg, there's someone out there," she said. "Right outside the window, looking at us."

"Is it him?" Megan asked, trying not to sound frightened. She didn't see any faces in the window, but she didn't want to keep waiting in the dark, so she decided to take the initiative and opened the front door to investigate herself. Her head moved to the right, then to the left, then shot back to the right.

"What the...? Dianne, was that here when we first came inside?" Megan pointed at something as she stood halfway out of the door.

Dianne got up from the chair and went over to her sister. Leaning her head out into the rain, she made out a wheelchair parked against the window. No one sat in it, like it had rolled out of nowhere, appearing out of thin air. "I don't remember. It could've been there before. I don't know."

"Todd?" Megan yelled out. "Where are you?"

Only the thunder replied.

Lightning flashed.

"He should've taken us with him," Megan added.

The sisters returned inside and shut the door. Megan ran over to the phone, her frantic fingers fidgeting with every moving piece.

In her struggle to make a call, Megan noticed the long white wire coming from the bottom of the phone's base. She followed it with her eyes, pulling it along until her stomach dropped. The wire didn't extend to the outlet. Someone had snipped it as tinier, frayed wires shot out of the end. Even if the power came back or the phone lines were fixed, the rotary phone was useless.

"All right," Megan said after chucking the phone into the corner behind the reception desk. It crashed like the thunder overhead. "Let's get the hell out of here. This is just stupid—one broken phone. The security guard didn't give us a cell phone and was of no help to us. Let's just go, ok? Forget Todd and this whole broken-down place. If you're good to walk, we're gonna keep going until we find actual help. I don't even know why we allowed ourselves to come inside."

Her panic and desperation had made her walk through the open gate with her sister and put her trust in the guard. What else was she supposed to do? Wait outside?

"We're just gonna run straight out of here, right to the front gate," Megan said. "Are you ready? Are you sure you're good to go?"

Dianne nodded. Adrenaline pumped through her veins. "Yeah, but how are we going to get through the gate?"

"We'll break the thing down if we have to," Megan said as she walked over to the door again, grabbing the handle. "One way or another, we're leaving. We're finding a way out before things get any worse."

There was no further discussion, no countdown. Megan opened the door to the Administration Building and ran out into the storm with her sister close behind.

Chapter 3

The Flashlight

The rain fell sideways in thick drops as Megan and Dianne raced to the front gate of the hospital. The concrete paths were slick, and the overgrown grass was soaked and weighed down from the storm.

Dianne felt eyes on her as they ran. Not just one set but many, following their movements from all over the grounds and beyond the dark and looming windows of the big brick buildings surrounding them.

When the sisters reached the rusted gate, Megan immediately started yanking and shaking the bars, making the gate wiggle. She grabbed the center locking piece and pulled hard but couldn't loosen it.

Dianne went into the booth beside the gate, trying to find a lever or button that would open the old thing up. She remembered seeing Todd using a key to open the gate. Then again, even if she *did* have the key, would it would work since the power went dead? It was just another layer of misfortune added to the horrific night. All she could do was feel around the small table, painting her fingers in dust.

Outside, Megan attempted to climb up the bars. The

gate stood tall and slippery, with the heavy rain spilling down the rusted metal. Droplets danced off her jacket and soaked her stomach through her torn shirt. She couldn't get up more than a foot off the ground before she had to let go and rub her elbow.

"There has to be another way out of here," Dianne said as she left the booth. "The entrance and exit can't be the same place."

The thunder growled above.

Lightning lit up the hospital grounds.

Eyes continued to stare from places unseen.

"Where did Todd go?" Megan asked. "I say we go find him and force him to let us out of here."

The Band-Aid on Dianne's temple loosened from the rain. She felt the sticky parts losing their grip against her skin. She looked back toward the Administration Building and the other buildings to the right of it. Dianne could only see by squinting through the rain. "Didn't he say the generator wasn't far behind the Administration Building?"

"I think so," Megan said. "Let's go get him before we drown in this weather."

With fast but careful steps, the sisters ran in the other direction, staying on the concrete paths that went around the grounds. They ran by a few hidden benches among the grass. Dianne almost tripped over one of the legs that poked out. Then, Megan kicked aside an IV pole that lay across the path around the Administration Building. Meanwhile, the number of watching eyes seemed to multiply. Every step she took, Dianne sensed a growing audience watching their every move.

Two buildings stood to the sisters' right side. A white light sat on the ground on the line between the concrete and the high grass as they rounded the Administration Building.

It shone off to the side toward the chain-link fence with barbed wire on the top. Dianne wondered if this place was more a prison than a hospital and whether there *would* be another way out.

"Todd?" Megan said as she and her sister approached the light. "Where are you?"

No answer came through the rain.

"We want out of here!" she added.

Dianne approached the light. She knelt to pick up a fat metal flashlight, more vintage than any kind she'd held before. It was heavy and appeared to be the one Todd held when he found them. "Todd?"

With the guiding beam, Dianne and Megan saw across the grass at the small brick building with a sign that read: GUARD POST. Beside it was a caged-in space with wires leaving from a large black and red box. Knobs and levers were on the side, with a faint orange light coming from the top.

"The generator!" Megan said.

"But where's Todd?" Dianne asked before she shot the flashlight around, illuminating the patches of tall grass and the side of the building labeled WING A that stood to the left of the guard post.

"Maybe he's in there," Megan said, motioning to the post. "C'mon."

Moving along the path, the sisters looked at the powered-down generator. Dianne wondered what happened to the security guard. Another missing person. First, the old woman in the car. Now, the security guard. Two people vanished, and two sisters trapped in an abandoned mental hospital, all in one night. The guard post provided Megan and Dianne with cover from the rain. Their bodies shook, dripping wet with their clothes soaked all the way through. Water sloshed in their shoes. Soon their adrenaline wouldn't be enough to keep their bodies warm.

Dianne shined the light around the post, finding the space similar to that of a tollbooth on the turnpike and the little building by the front gate. It was tight and had a single desk littered with papers, a calendar covered with scribbles and coffee stains. Beside it sat an overfilled trash can with what looked like balled-up tissues and crumpled cigarette packs. The scent of expired tobacco and must hung in the air.

"Doesn't look like there's a phone in here," Dianne said.

"Probably wouldn't matter if there was," Megan said. "How could anyone work in here? It's a dump. This whole place is." She leaned over the desk that looked out of a small window that faced the generator outside and started to search the drawers. Dianne scooted behind her.

On the far wall hung a small metal box with a key dangling from the lock. Dianne approached it and used slow hands to turn the key and pull the lid open. Inside the metal box were rows of bronze keys. Some hung in stacks, while others were by themselves, dangling all alone on their hooks. Dianne shined her light close to them, trying to make out what their labels said as they all shared the same weathered appearance. The lettering on the top of the keys was faded, rubbed away by time. She made out a W on one and a capital B on another. One read QUARTERS but the word that preceded it was gone. Her eyes traveled, looking for a key for the front gate's mechanism.

Megan dug through more stacks of paper as she explored the drawers. Pens. Paperclips. Big erasers. Stamps. Nothing of any use. It wasn't until she searched the second, bigger drawer below that she found a walkie-talkie. Megan pulled it out and held it up, yanking out the stubborn collapsed antenna on top. Rust wrapped around the silver base as she extended it outward. A dial sat on the front with a button on the side of the plastic casing.

"Hello? Hello?" Megan said into the speaker as she played with the knob and pressed down on the side button. "Can anyone hear me?"

No sounds came, not even static. Megan threw the walkie-talkie over her shoulder and continued searching the drawer, feeling around for anything else.

Dianne was making a small collection of keys in her palm. She kept the ones that had the clearest wording. She had one for Wing A. Wing B. One of the QUARTERS keys, and a mysterious one with EN------E on it.

In the back of the bottom drawer, Megan's fingers met a bulb. Batteries. Big ones. She slid everything out, finding a flashlight lens attached to a red box with a handle on top. Megan pulled it out, having to get a good grip on the heavy piece of equipment.

"Look at this old thing," Megan said before she found the switch on the side. The light in the big bulb flickered for a second until an orangish light appeared, illuminating the back of Dianne. "Wow, I can't believe it actually works."

Dianne turned from the box of keys to see not only Megan looking at her, but an elderly man standing in the doorway, gazing at her with eyes as tired and low as an old dog. Dianne gasped and dropped her handful of keys to the floor where they clattered. Her back bumped into the box of keys on the wall, making them fall from their hooks and join the others below as they all bounced, jingling on the concrete.

Megan snapped her body around, almost knocking out the old man with her heavy boxed flashlight. She used both hands to hold up her light as she backed closer to her sister. Together, their trembling lights illuminated the man.

"Who are you?" Megan asked, her voice shaking.

Wet, white hair matted the sides of the old man's liver-spotted head. His skin hung long and saggy, and the red vest he wore over an untucked dress shirt was stained with more than just drops of rain. His khakis, too. The filth of rain and dirt dripped onto his tan, mud-covered Velcro shoes.

His mouth moved, opening and closing as he stared into the lights like a deer facing a tractor-trailer barreling toward it.

"What are you doing out here?" Megan asked the old man. "Where did you come from?"

"I-I-I—" The old man stuttered. His lips wagged. "I-I-I was l-l-l-looking to get back to my b-b-bed."

"Your bed?" Megan said, almost starting to laugh at this complete absurdity. Her mental state was clearly breaking down. "Sir, how could you have a bed around here? This place is—"

"My-my-my nurse. Claire. She was taking me for a walk when it started to r-r-r-r-rain. She left me out here all by myself."

Silence fell inside the guard post, leaving only the sound of the thunder and rain outside. Megan and Dianne stared at the old man as he held his eyes on Dianne before shifting them over to Megan. The lights didn't seem to bother his cloudy blue eyes.

"Have you seen Todd anywhere?" Megan asked. "Maybe he can help you. He's the security guard. We're not from around here. We're actually trying to get out."

The old man shook his head, wagging his flabby neck at the girls.

"Do you know how we can get out of this place? My

sister and I are in a lot of pain from our car accident, and we can't stay here," Megan said.

The old man didn't shake his head. He just stood with his mouth hanging open, exposing his crooked teeth. One was missing on the side of the top row. "I could help you, but only if you take me to my bed and have Claire draw me a bath. I have to get out of this rain."

"Ok," Megan said, trying to work with the stuttering old man. "All right, we can get you to your bed. You just have to tell us where to take you."

The old man shook his head and said, "Tha-that's the thing. I've forgotten where my r-room is. Much like you two, I'm l-lo-lo-los—" He continued to struggle with the word as his hands shook like leaves. His whole body began to contort.

Megan and Dianne froze. The old man stood in front of the door, filling up the entire frame. There was no clear path for the sisters to escape.

"It's ok, we understand," Dianne said, attempting to calm the man down. "Just take a deep breath."

The old man stopped trying to speak and let his body get the shakes out. With his arms twisting and his hands trembling, the sisters noticed a bracelet that slid out from his sleeve and down his wrist. A faded white strip with black writing on it.

"What's that there?" Megan asked, shining her light on the old man's wrinkled wrist. "What's that say?"

The old man shook his head. "My eyes don't work like they used to. I don't have my glasses. Please help me."

Dianne said, "It's ok. I'm just gonna take a look at it." Megan kept close beside her as Dianne went up to the old man and read the bracelet aloud. "Gerald M. Swaggart. Room two twenty-one. A Wing."

"Yes, that sounds right," Gerald said. His eyes were closed. "It's coming back to me now. I'm G-G-G-G—"

"Shh, it's ok," Dianne said. She turned to Megan, who was staring at Gerald with irritated eyes, like she was so offended at the sight of the trembling man. "I think it's just outside here. We can take him to his room and maybe get out that way. Maybe through a window or another exit."

"Are you serious?" Megan said. Although the night was out of control, her tone came off as rude in front of Gerald. Dianne didn't feel much different but was not willing to brush strangers aside like that. She still felt sick from what happened with the old woman in the car.

"What else are we supposed to do?" Dianne said. "This man needs our help, and we need his if he can tell us how to get out of here."

"This is crazy, just crazy. I mean...what are we doing?" Megan faced Gerald, taking in his frightened, messy appearance. "Where did you even *come* from? Are you a squatter or something? Is this whole place another 'haunted' attraction, and you're an actor? Is Todd an actor?"

"Meg...," Dianne said under her breath.

"I mean, Jesus, we almost died out there, our car is crushed, you're bleeding from your head, my arm's probably broken! We've lost the old woman, Todd, and now we have this man standing before us. What do you think is gonna happen to him? How much do you wanna bet he's going to disappear too? We take him to his 'room,' and then we're trapped there until another person pops out to scare us?"

"I don't know," Dianne said, raising her voice. "I don't know!"

Gerald began to shake again as tears welled in his eyes. His voice trembled, more so than before. "I'm sorry. I didn't mean to..."

Dianne placed her hand on her head, exhausted.

"All right," Megan said with a sigh. "I'll just have to play along. Let's take Gerald," she turned to him, "if that even *is* your real name. But it doesn't matter. Dianne's right, we don't have any other choice. We might as well continue along with this crazy ride until we drop dead, right? What's the worst that could happen? I'm just hoping this is all some prank gone wrong, an elaborate haunted ghost tour with hidden cameras."

Gerald tried to say thank you through his sobs. He nodded his head as it shook. In the light of the flashlights, his liver spots looked darker than before, like they were changing shades as he stood in front of the door.

Megan blew air out from her nose. "Yeah, if this is a sick joke, I'm gonna murder whoever's behind it."

"That's enough, Meg," Dianne said before turning her attention back to Gerald. "Are you able to walk?"

"Yes, I should be able to make it as long as we go soon. The r-r-r-rain is not good for my joints," Gerald said.

Dianne shined her light down on the floor until she found the key labeled A WING with the letter G halfway gone. Her heart jumped—in her anxiety, she'd forgotten to grab the other set of keys off the concrete.

"I hope Todd comes back and gets the power back on, unless that's not part of the script," Megan snapped. "My God, back into the storm we go."

Chapter 4

The Second Floor

The cold, stormy night remained unapologetic as Megan and Dianne walked on either side of Gerald toward the double doors on the far-right side of the Wing A building. Beside them stood the tall chain-link and barbed wire fence with a fine layer of chipped rust covering the metal, a perfect texture to keep the girls and their new acquaintance trapped inside the grounds.

An awning hung above the side doors to the wing, giving the three of them cover from the storm. Dianne pulled both doors, finding them to be locked tight. She slid the faded bronze key into the small lock on the right door. It went in without a fight and turned until a little click came from the hole. She took the key out and put it in her pocket before opening the door wide, holding it open for Gerald and her sister to enter.

Inside, the three of them stood before a stairwell between brick walls covered in various colors of layered graffiti spray that displayed big, illegible bubbled words and satanic-looking symbols. A devil's head and a hidden pentagram between a depiction of Jesus on the cross. Gang signs. Through the smeared paint, Dianne made out the words, "God has left this place." A naked woman with her eyes X-ed out in red was painted next to it.

"Wow," Megan whispered.

"This place is all I know," Gerald said.

The air smelled stale, and a slight chill hung around. Ahead of them stood another set of double doors. The sisters' flashlights shined toward the windows on them, but it was too dark beyond for their lights to reach.

"Can you make it up the stairs?" Dianne asked.

Gerald nodded. "I just have to go s-s-slow."

"That's fine. Take your time," Dianne said. "We'll be right behind you."

Gerald grabbed onto the filthy handrail and started his ascent. Every time he bent his knees to move up to the next step, his joints cracked. The old man sounded like his bones were about to break with every movement. Gerald still didn't complain as he climbed to the top. He only uttered words under his breath that the sisters couldn't understand, but they didn't bother him as they let him make it to the second-floor landing without incident.

There was no handle on the door labeled with a faded 2 at the top of the stairs, but Dianne forced it open with a shove. The door creaked on its aged hinges as the three of them walked through and entered the long hallway.

The graffiti continued to cover the walls and the doors to the patient rooms that went along the hall. Trash littered the floor. A hospital bed lay sideways among the garbage with its mattress cut and gutted.

Room 230 was the first room, or last room, depending on which side of the hallway you entered, that stood with a big red X spray-painted on the wooden door. The knob was cracked off, leaving a little piece of silver left to dangle. The thin window on the door was cracked.

"What's his room number?" Megan asked without an ounce of patience in her voice.

"Two twenty-one," Dianne replied.

"All right. Let's just get him to it," Megan said before quickening her pace. She waved her light left and right, not wasting any time as she walked farther down the dark and littered hallway. Another fallen IV pole rolled across the floor. Megan had to kick it away before she tripped. "And see what our next obstacle will be!"

Rain pattered on the roof, except for where there were gaping holes in the ceiling, which allowed droplets to splash across the floor. Lightning flashed outside, each strike momentarily lighting the way.

Gerald and Dianne moved down the hall. Dianne tried not to peek into any of the other rooms in fear of what would be looking back at her, so she kept her beam facing forward to help guide Gerald as they shuffled along.

"Here," Megan said, her heavy light aiming at the placard. "Room 221, right where Mr. Gerald needs to be." She kicked open the graffiti-ridden door.

"Meg, wait a second," Dianne said.

"I'm coming," Gerald added, picking up his pace a little. Dianne noticed dirt falling from him, dirty rain rolling off him like he was melting. Megan stood in the doorway, scanning the nasty room. The ceiling fell apart as holes brought in streams of rain. More holes were in the floor, looking down into whatever room sat below, some big enough to fall through, others as small as bullet holes. In the corner, next to a trashed bathroom, a metal bed frame sat with a shredded mattress on top—sheets with big red and brown marks on them. Leather straps sat on the floor next to broken jars surrounded by soil; dead plants. A barred window looked out to the hospital grounds.

Gerald and Dianne made it to 221, and Gerald couldn't seem more delighted. He walked into the tarnished room, approaching the side of the bed as if there wasn't total decay all around him. *Maybe he was a squatter?*

"So, could you please tell us how to get out here now?" Megan asked. "We've given you all the help we can."

Gerald, who was about to sit down on the edge of the disgusting mattress, said, "W-w-w-wait, what about my bath? Have you told Claire to draw me a b-b-bath?"

"We don't know where she is," Megan said. "You'll just have to wait for her to come back."

Gerald's wet face dropped. His eyebrows curled in a sudden depression. "But I'm awfully cold and filthy."

The familiar feeling of being watched came over Dianne again. Eyes were on her and her sister, and not just Gerald's.

"She'll come for you," Dianne said reassuringly, like she was the old man's mother. "But my sister and I really need to be going."

"Oh..." Gerald shuffled toward the girls, who stood in the doorway with their lights trained on him. "You're leaving me? The visit is over?"

"Yes!" Megan said, not covering up her impatience. "Can't you see we're hurt and totally soaked? We brought you to your room, now tell us how to get out of here!"

Without acknowledging Megan's tone, Gerald said, "Maybe you two could draw me a ba-ba-ba-bath. Would you do that for me?"

Megan began to turn away from the room. "C'mon, Dianne. I'm done with these people. Let's break out ourselves. No one in this place is gonna help us."

Suddenly, Gerald snapped. His voice rose to new volumes.

"No!" he cried out before throwing himself forward, pulling Dianne backward into the room with surprising strength. Gerald's hands lunged for Megan, who was out in the hallway, backing away from the crazed man. "You can't leave me now!"

"Don't touch me!" Megan shouted.

Dianne moved toward her sister to get between her and Gerald when the door to his room shut with such force, she felt the wind coming off it. The lock above the handle turned and clicked from the outside. She yanked and pulled on the handle as she saw Megan struggle with the old man in the hallway through the tiny window on the door.

"You're all I have," Gerald cried as his trembling hands grabbed for Megan. "Pl-pl-pl-pl-please!"

"Dianne!" Megan shouted.

"I can't get out!" Dianne pounded her fist on the little window. "The door's stuck!"

"Just stay with me. I promise I'll be good!" Gerald pleaded.

Megan's flashlight swayed, the ray of light illuminating the right side of the hall, where multiple people watched the brawl. Folks with pale faces were leaning out of the other rooms, staring through the darkness, unmoving. Men and women of all ages and races. Watching. Megan's attention remained fixated on Gerald as she flung the fat flashlight upward, crashing it into Gerald's chest, making him explode into a thick cloud of dust in an instant. His clothes, skin, everything transformed into nothing but a dirty mist, like brown ashes. Gerald M. Swaggart was no more.

"Meg!" Dianne shouted from inside the room as the murky cloud covered the window, blocking her view. She tried to shine her light against the glass, but it only reflected in her face.

With the weight of Megan's vintage flashlight high in the air, Megan tumbled backward, falling inside the room across 221. The flashlight fell from her grip and crashed onto the floor, shattering the lens but not the bulb as the orange glow remained.

A plume of floating brown dust flew into her nose and mouth, making her choke for a moment. Her eyes watered as she tried to blink out the itch. Megan attempted to get back up to run to her sister, but the door shut and locked itself before she could take a step. Her body bounced off the hard wooden door, sending her back down to the ground.

"Meg! Meg, can you hear me?" Dianne shouted from 221. "Megan!"

Megan lifted herself from the floor and began pounding on the door. Kicks came soon after, but it seemed her strength was no match for the steel hinges and lock. Out of all the things in the broken-down and rotting old hospital, the doors of Wing A's second floor were sealed tight.

"Dianne," Megan said before having another coughing fit. Dirt and dust clung to the glass of the door's window. "Dianne, I'm stuck! Are you out there?" Just like her sister, Megan was sealed inside, screaming and banging on the door while being blinded by the floating dust.

On either side of the hall, the Willis sisters shouted for each other, crying into the dark. They only heard each other's faint voices that sounded like whispers floating through a long tunnel as the two of them were trapped in their own separate prisons.

Chapter 5

The Girl Who Believed

Dianne Willis was into ghosts and spirits. The afterlife. The powers of the universe and the energy that surrounds the living. Lightness and darkness. Positivity and negativity. She wasn't religious, she didn't follow the Bible or attend any churches but instead subscribed to the ideology of what is known as "New Age." The belief in souls and spirituality that goes well beyond the lessons of God or Jesus Christ.

Dianne believed that there were different planes of existence. If you were a good person and gave off positive vibes, your soul would ultimately become one with the universe. After you die, you'd either come back to this world via reincarnation or ascend to the astral realm, where you'd be crystallized among the stars of the galaxy and merge among the other waves of celestial souls.

On the other hand, if you were a bad person and had negative energy around you and coming out of your thoughts, you'd turn into some sort of demon or dark entity that lived between the dimensions where you'd rub elbows with other monsters.

It was all about how you manifested the energies of life, how you handled the ever-present powers you couldn't see.

If you asked her, Dianne would tell you she came to this universal energy and spiritual conclusion not only from watching countless hours of YouTube videos but from experiencing it firsthand. Whether it was using the power of positive thinking to manifest certain situations and people into her life or getting experimental with an Ouija board with her friends, Dianne had seen some things that changed her whole perception of reality.

For example, there was a guy in one of her high school classes who she liked. Jason Tanner, a sort of nerdy-rocker type who always caught Dianne's eye when he walked into class. He seemed so interesting to her with his spiked hair and giant glasses. Unique. Creative in an attractive way she couldn't quite describe.

She hadn't ever spoken to him, and he sat on the opposite side of the room, as physically far away from her as possible, but after Dianne practiced "positive visualization" and focused hard on a scenario of running into Jason somewhere, her fantasy manifested itself into real life.

Dianne was a member of a poetry club that met once a week on Wednesday evenings in the back of the school's library. It was a small group consisting of only five members overall; four girls and one boy named Kevin, a theater student who enjoyed the practice of prose. In every meeting, they would talk and share the work they had written from the past week. Their emotional messages. The life experiences that went into the poems. Nothing out of the ordinary most of the time. That was until Jason Tanner showed up during one of the meetings, asking if it was okay that he wanted to join despite the school year being halfway through. He also confessed how much he'd been wanting to share some of his pieces and express himself.

Dianne didn't believe it at first. Her brain tried to rationalize it as a coincidence, but in her heart, she knew there was something to the power of the mind. Visualizations. Energy. The situation was just too odd and perfect for it to have happened naturally. No one at school gave much of a hoot about poetry, and now here was the guy who Dianne desired to meet, the dude who sat at the far end of the sophomore year psychology class, confessing his love of the craft of poetry in front of the tiniest club in school.

Of course, Dianne got to talk to Jason and get to know him both in and out of the group meetings. There were times it was just the two of them for the night, seeing a movie or grabbing a bite to eat. It never blossomed into a full-on relationship, but Dianne was beyond satisfied. Not only had she manifested a new, fun friend, but she unlocked something deep in her spiritual mind. The power of positive energy. The ability to bring her fantasies out of her dreams and make them reality.

As one could imagine, Dianne didn't stop there. She used this visualization method to meet more people, make new friends, go on dates, get better grades, and have an overall better feeling about her life's progression. When times were tough, she turned her mind toward the course of positivity. She dabbled in crystals. Vision boards. Listening to uplifting ambient music on her phone. Dianne did all this to soak her soul in the waters of spiritual enlightenment.

But you can't have the good without the bad. Light without dark. Up without down.

With her proof of positive affirmations, Dianne was too curious not to dive into the darker side of energies, the nightmares that lurk not far from the brighter dreams.

Before all of this, Dianne already believed in ghosts. As a child, she had numerous experiences with the paranormal, the unexplainable. Shadows running down the hall of her childhood home. Faces appearing through windows. Voices in the night. There was one time she saw a woman in an old dress appear before her very eyes, glowing green from head to toe with wild hair shooting out like a broom. That was her most vivid, most terrifying experience, at least before she entered Shaded Grove.

The idea of demons, or entities more sinister than ghosts, was something she thought only existed for religious folks. Being raised in a secular, liberal household in Central Pennsylvania, Dianne only discovered the otherworldly monsters after using a Ouija board and found herself sitting in her living room with long scratches on her back. She promised herself she'd never do it again, but the horrific night she and her friends contacted demonic forces didn't stop her further research on the subject. More YouTube videos. Wikipedia pages. Forums. There was no question that evil energy lingered not far from humanity.

Yes, Dianne was tapped into spiritual warfare. Good versus evil on a universal level. However, her beliefs were hers alone. No one else in her family seemed to agree with her on the topics of ghosts and demons, especially not her older sister, Megan.

Dianne's mom, Deborah Willis, entertained the idea of Heaven and Hell, but didn't take it too seriously. While she understood the concept of demonic monsters and spirits trapped between this realm and the afterlife, she was lost when it came to dimensions and astral projection. It was just a rabbit hole Deborah didn't want to go down.

However, despite her inability to share in Dianne's passion, that didn't stop Deborah from allowing her daughter to go on ghost tours, see psychics, and venture to any supposedly haunted location. She supported Dianne's interests, even if she wasn't on board with all of it. As long as Dianne kept the course and kept her grades up, she could dabble in any extracurricular activity she pleased. Besides, according to Deborah, nothing could be scarier than *her* parents and how she was raised back in the day. "Real, old-fashioned fear," as Deborah put it. To her, the wild and aggressive parenting of the previous generation was far more frightening than any soldier of Satan's army, or Victorian-era spirit. Perhaps that's why Deborah didn't talk too much about her parents and kept things short when it came to discussing her childhood.

Well, that may hold true for Dianne's mother, but to Dianne, she'd take a rage-filled grandpa or scowling grandma any day over another second trapped in a room of an abandoned mental hospital, not that there was anything abandoned about it at this point. But Dianne wasn't a fool. She knew what this was, what these mysterious people, or rather spirits, were all about. The issue was, why wouldn't they let her out? What were these spirits trying to do with her and Megan? Dianne didn't think of herself as a bad person, she hardly ever gave off negative energy, and she was as nice to the spirits of the old hospital as she could be. Sure, she could see how Megan kept being difficult, being hostile toward the folks that roamed the grounds, but she ultimately helped and played along. Megan wasn't the aggressor, she just reacted, not believing in the things that were happening to her, not truly seeing the faces of the phantoms for what they were.

Now, as Dianne continued to punch the locked door of Room 221, she wondered what was happening out in the hallway, in the other rooms of the second floor, and if her sister made it out of the scrap in one piece.

"Meg, what happened?" Dianne shouted. "Are you ok?"

Megan responded, but her voice was too faint to decipher the words. She sounded far away, like the walls were thicker than the brick that built the place back in God knows when.

The room fell cold from the night's rain that dripped down from the holes in the ceiling. Dianne searched around for something she could use to smash through the window on the door.

Everything was soiled and rusted.

Maybe this would work, Dianne thought, eyeing a piece of a broken jar on the floor. *No. I can't risk cutting myself. I could get an infection.*

After a few moments of scanning with her light, Dianne went for the leather straps, which sat by a hole in the floor not far from the rusted bed frame. The leather was brown with splotches of black stains. The buckles were crusty.

With one hand on the flashlight and the other gripping the end of the leather strap, Dianne approached the door. She swung the strap back before whipping it forward, smashing the buckle against the wood beside the glass. She winded up again, this time making contact with the window but not having any luck cracking it.

Again.

Again.

Dianne worked the leather strap, whipping it harder with each thrust, finding no success in breaking out. The glass barely chipped from the attempts.

She next used the end of the flashlight's handle. Dianne thought that would surely do the trick but found no success. The window wouldn't budge.

"Meg, are you still out there?" Dianne asked with her face against the door. She heard a faint voice answer. The words faded, too far away to be understood. Tears of panic welled in her eyes. Her hands trembled. Nausea came over her. "I'm gonna try to get out of here! Just stay wherever you are!"

Dianne turned from the door and ran to the window that looked out over the hospital grounds outside with black metal bars just beyond. The rain slowed as it fell and spilled on the glass. Dianne pounded on it with her fists before resorting to the leather strap. She found the same results as she did with the window on the door—little chips. No cracks. Whoever designed this place must've been sure to make the windows and doors unbreakable.

She moved around the room frantically. Without being able to break through the windows, there weren't many options left. Dianne searched for vents or anything she could crawl through until she returned to the spot where she found the leather straps, where a hole in the floor under the filthy mattress and rusty bed frame exposed a room downstairs.

Using her sneakers, Dianne kicked the bed frame out from against the wall until she had enough space to see the entire hole. It wasn't huge, but just wide enough for Dianne to look down with her light.

In the flashlight's beam, Dianne saw the room below. Shelves. Papers scattered everywhere. Boxes. Broken glass. A telephone smashed on the floor. There weren't any bodies or anyone that Dianne could see.

"Hello?" she said. "Is anyone down there?"

No response.

Dianne sighed and wiped away the wet hair that dangled in front of her eyes. She carefully moved her body backward, lowering her feet into the hole, swinging them slightly to the left and right, hoping to find leverage on top of one of the shelves in the middle of the room. She shimmied herself farther downward until her arms started to shake as she dangled with most of her body down the hole. Dianne tried to ease herself more, but she was too weak to keep her body up, and her hands slid across the crusty, rusty floor of 221 until she fell all the way through.

The fall wasn't too far down, but it still made Dianne shriek when she landed on her side on a cardboard box on the tiled floor. Her body rolled for a second, bumping into one of the shelves. It wobbled for a moment until it leaned back and fell, crashing into another shelf standing behind it. A loud smashing sound came as the metal scaffolding collided and sent all the contents on their shelves flying about. Pieces of paper danced in the dark. Bottles shattered into one another. Boxes exploded with folders sliding out of them.

The domino effect of the shelving accident eventually left the room silent, with a fresh cloud of dust hanging in the air. Luckily, Dianne's flashlight survived the fall and crash. She grabbed it off the ground as she covered her mouth and coughed, waving away the dirty particles that filled the atmosphere of the small room, which looked to be a file storage area. It didn't have the grittiness of the room upstairs.

Dianne got up, feeling a slight twinge of pain on her left arm and leg. There was no question that she would be bruised and battered once this was all over. The only question was how far her mind and body would take her through this nightmare.

Papers and manila folders were under her shoes. Various names stared back up at her on the labels. She spent a moment or two searching for *Gerald M. Swaggart* among the mess of documents but found nothing on the man.

In the corner sat a desk with a typewriter on top of it. Beside it, another window with black bars outside. It was too dark outside to see if anyone was out on the grounds. She wondered where Todd had gone off to or if he ever returned to the Administration Building.

Dianne turned around and saw the door to the room. She went up to it and, of course, found it to be locked. However, there was a turn-lock above the handle. As opposed to the doors upstairs that locked on the outside, this room locked on the inside. Dianne twisted the lock and escape the smelly room.

On the first floor of Wing A, Dianne saw the hall was in even worse shape than the one upstairs. The first floor had more graffiti, more trash. Wheelchairs parked and flipped all along the walls. Beds thrown to the side. Papers littering the tiles. IV bags, both empty and filled with blood and mysterious liquids that didn't look safe for human veins.

Dianne felt as vulnerable as ever as she shined her flash-light down the left side of the hallway, illuminating not only what looked to be a nurse's station and a set of elevators but the back of a nurse who was walking with a patient toward the other end. She couldn't see their faces, but Dianne could tell the patient was twitching. His head was trembling. It sort of looked like Gerald, but not quite. He didn't have the same liver spots or red sweater. Perhaps the nurse that guided him through the pitch-black was Claire, the nurse who was supposed to draw Gerald's bath.

Either way, Dianne didn't say a word and started to walk the other way, trying not to make a sound as she quick-stepped toward the right side of the hall where she believed the stairwell sat. If she could get back to those stairs, she could retrace her steps back to where she last saw Megan before the sudden dust storm blocked her view.

Voices floated down the hall, bouncing off the walls. As Dianne traveled toward the double doors at the end, she heard weeping. The cries of a woman hidden behind one of the several doors that lined either side. A man shouting. Someone was sick, vomiting in the distance. A shriek echoed over the air. Punches rattled a door right beside Dianne, making her jump. She had to cover her mouth with her hand to stifle a scream. Terror chilled her spine as she waited for the door to explode and for whoever it was on the other side to break out and take her. The thought made her quick steps turn into a full-blown sprint.

Her flashlight's beam waved across the walls, illuminating the satanic symbols and gang graffiti in fast flashes. Her heart hammered against her chest, and she had to take quick breaths to keep her stamina up. Although her body had already gone through so much, the new shot of adrenaline coursing through her veins gave her an extra push to continue running. It was only a matter of time until she passed out or collapsed on the floor.

At the end of the hall, Dianne found the double doors. She moved so fast from the hallway that she used her momentum to push through them with her elbow. The creaky doors flung open, and Dianne found herself back in the cold stairwell again, except this time, things were a little different than before.

When Dianne rounded the bottom of the stairs, she saw that the steps leading up to the second floor were almost destroyed. There were three steps, a giant hole, and the remaining two steps up to the landing. It was like a wrecking ball had come down and smashed the steps into oblivion not long after Dianne, Megan, and Gerald climbed them.

"Shit," Dianne said to herself. "What the…?"

The handrail was gone from the destruction, so the only way Dianne would get up to the second floor would be to jump across the hole and grab the ledge or return to the first-floor hallway and hope the elevators were operational in a power outage. That, or travel to the opposite end of the floor and hope there was another stairwell beyond the ghost nurse and patient. Not only them, but the hall of shouting horrors and mysterious patients locked away behind rattling doors.

Dianne stood on the edge of the bottom step, thinking about how she would jump to the top ledge, when she heard voices coming from the double doors she'd recently run through. They were loud, deep voices—men's voices shouting out into the dark. A woman cried. Dianne heard footsteps marching toward the stairwell.

"No, no, no," she said to herself. Her whole body shook as fresh fear found its way to her. It brought another shock of adrenaline into her veins, so much so that Dianne didn't waste another second and shoved her flashlight into the waistband of her jeans. She jumped off the bottom steps with her arms extended outwards.

Her arms landed on the concrete above, the edge of the last step tucked under her elbows. The landing hurt, but Dianne didn't have time to consider it as she heard the double doors open below. The echo of the voices filled the stairwell with shrieks and cries of the mentally ill.

Dianne pulled herself up, but as she was about to swing her legs onto the landing, hands grabbed her feet and yanked her down. She felt fingers wrap around her ankles.

"Get off me!" she shouted.

Dianne kicked her legs, thrashing them as the hands reached for her. The flashlight in her waistband shot all around, but Dianne couldn't see who was trying to pull her down.

The voices weren't coherent. Only the sounds of pain rose in the darkness. Suffering. Agony.

Dianne's body slid an inch or two toward the edge until she gave another strong kick that lessened the grips around her ankles and ceased the shrieks below. The second she felt free, she swung her legs up and over the hanging step until she rolled toward the second-floor door. On her back, she took heavy breaths and grabbed her chest. Her eyes were closed tight. She wanted to snap her eyes open and find herself sitting in the passenger seat of her sister's Ford as they continued their drive home. She wanted to feel the wave of relief that this whole scenario in Shaded Grove was nothing more than a nightmare.

But there was no waking from the bad dream. As much as positive thinking and visualization worked for talking to a cute guy in school or getting a good grade on a mid-term paper, it wasn't doing too much for Dianne at the moment. It was too bad one's thoughts didn't manifest immediately. If that were the case, Dianne and Megan would already be miles from this place. Back home. Safe. Talking about the Ashford House ghost tour, telling their mother how creepy it was. Well, Dianne would be anyway. Megan would prob- ably be "debunking" all the paranormal experiences that went down in the haunted house. As always.

Dianne got up from the floor of the landing and took the flashlight out of her jeans. Shining the light over the edge, she saw nothing but a cloud of dust floating where the giant hole was in the staircase. No nurses. No patients. No one.

With her heart rate still sky-high, Dianne turned and

went through the door to the second floor, where she was met with the familiar graffiti, however, the hallway floor looked to have gone in the same direction as the stairs as holes spread out over the tiles. Dianne walked down the hall, but she had to be careful not to trip or fall. The hospital crumbled by the moment. For all she knew, her next step could be her last, and then it would be back down into the first floor of terror for another runaround. Then again, who's to say that the floor downstairs wouldn't fall apart and expose a basement level? Dianne didn't even want to know what waited all the way underground. If the energy felt dark up here, there was no telling what she'd feel the farther down she went.

Room 221 was right where Dianne left it, shut and locked about halfway down the hall. The cloud of dust still lingered in the air, but not as dense. The dirt wasn't as blinding.

"Meg?" Dianne said. "Meg, where are you?"

For a moment, no response came. Then, just as Dianne was going to start shouting, a bang came from the door across from 221. Dianne snapped around and shined her light on the door for Room 222, which had a red cross sprayed on the wood and her sister's face up against the window.

"Meg!"

"I'm stuck in here," Megan said from beyond the glass, her eyes wide and terrified. Her voice sounded like she spoke through a tin can. "Can you open the door?"

Dianne grabbed the handle and pulled with all her might, but the door wouldn't open. Megan started pounding on the other side. The door was shut solid.

"Get away from the window," Megan said.

"What?" Megan asked. "What did you say?"

"I said, GET AWAY FROM THE WINDOW!"

Megan backed up a bit until Dianne started to smash the handle of her flashlight against the glass. "I already tried that. It doesn't work. I tried the other window, too. They're unbreakable! There's no way out of here!"

"Dammit!" Dianne's breath was getting short. Panic set in big time as her eyes began to sting with tears. "We have to get you out! There's gotta be a way!"

Megan shook her head. "Where did you go? Where were you?"

"I was stuck in the other room," Dianne said, motioning to 221 behind her. "I found a hole and got out. There are these people downstairs and these holes forming. This whole place is falling apart!"

"This is completely out of control," Megan said with her hands on her head. "I cannot believe this…"

Dianne pounded some more on the door to no avail.

"Wait. Do you still have that key? The one you used to get us in here?" Megan asked.

Dianne forgot all about that. The anxiety of the ever-changing night made her brain fuzzy.

"Yes, yes, I think so." Her hands shook as they dug into her pockets. In her right one, she found the brass key with faded letters on it. "Here!"

She shined her light down on the tiny lock above the handle. The key trembled as she tried to put it inside. No luck. The key couldn't even slide all the way through, no matter how hard Dianne pushed.

"It's not working!" Megan said.

All Dianne could do was shake her head as the hot tears in her eyes let loose and streamed down her face.

"C'mon!" Megan shouted. She slapped the window. "Why won't it work?"

Dianne pressed her head against the door in despair. She tried to think of anything she could do to save her sister, but it was so hard to focus. Too many emotions overwhelmed her.

"There has to be a key somewhere to open this," Megan said. "Even a crowbar."

Dianne swiped at her face before she looked on either side of the hallway. "I'm gonna keep looking until I find something to get you out of there. I hate to leave you here all alone, but I don't know what else to do."

Megan shrugged and shook her head.

"Are you okay? Do you feel all right enough in there?" Dianne asked.

"As all right as I can be," Megan replied. "It's not like I'm going anywhere or anyone's getting in. I don't even know what happened to Gerald. He just vanished, probably went the same way Todd did. Oh, Dianne... What a mess! I can't believe this is happening!"

Dianne knew these people were ghosts, but there wasn't any use trying to explain it all to her sister. Besides, Dianne didn't have all the answers herself. She had no control over the situation and had no authority to tell Megan how to handle spirits such as these. Their energy and behavior were unpredictable.

"There's a nurse's station downstairs. Maybe there's a key there or something to break the door off. I can check the other rooms, too," Dianne said with a shaky voice.

"And the power," Megan added. "Remember, there's that stupid generator out there. I have no clue how you'd turn it on, but maybe that has something to do with these doors. If not, you can get the gate open and run for help that way."

"Okay. Whatever it takes," Dianne cried.

Megan moved closer to the window and spoke with a voice that had more fear than anger. "Dianne, whatever you do, just be careful. I don't want you to get hurt or trapped. If you go down, both of us are as good as dead."

"Right..."

"I'm gonna keep trying to break out of here. If I can somehow, I'll come and find you. I still have my flashlight." Megan held up the heavy red box with the shattered lens. The orange glow came through the glass. "Although I almost broke the thing slamming it against the window."

Dianne nodded and said, "All right. I love you. I'm going to go as fast as I can. I promise."

"I love you, too," Megan said. "Watch yourself out there. Don't let any of these weirdos touch you."

"I won't," Dianne said before giving her sister one more look. She pressed her palm against the window and then turned away.

Chapter 6

The Girl Who Would Kill

Megan Willis was two years older than her sister, Dianne, but they looked like twins. They shared the same jet-black, slightly curly hair. The same dark-brown eyes. Both even had the same love for rock music and television dramas. However, their similarities ended there.

While Dianne was the quieter and more reserved of the two, Megan was loud and blunt. She didn't mind telling you how she felt, even if her rant was riddled with curse words and personal attacks. She had no issue telling a pursuing gentleman to get lost or flipping the bird to a cop who wasted her time. And once you got on her bad side, it was near impossible to get off it. She held a grudge and would take it all the way to her grave if you crossed her. It sounds harsh, but Megan's attitude stemmed from a combination of two things: her mother and her job.

Deborah Willis, being a single mother and a victim of multiple irresponsible men throughout her life, was a tough woman who also didn't take crap from anyone. Not only did she have to spend a childhood in a house filled with constant domestic issues, but she also spent many years of her adulthood wading through boyfriends and ultimately an ex-husband until she learned how to enjoy her own company without having to rely on a man to fill the void.

She did her best not to fill her daughters' youth with the same stress she experienced, but, of course, there's no way to eradicate all of life's ripples. No matter what, children are going to feel the psychological effects of divorce. New men coming and going. It's all observed and permanently marked on their minds, and when you're a parent, there's only so much you can say to try to fix a fractured soul, especially when yours is in pieces, too.

In Megan's case, she was forever scarred by what she witnessed in her house. How different guys would treat her mother, scream at her, call her no good. They'd abuse alcohol, cause a ruckus, throw things, stuff like that. Megan wondered how her mom consistently attracted such vile men, especially ones like Scott.

Scott was one of those guys who seemed well-to-do, a salt-of-the-earth kind of fellow who worked blue-collar jobs and tinkered with old cars. He had thinning hair and a bushy black beard. When Megan first met him, she didn't like him, but couldn't quite understand why. Despite Scott's easy-going attitude, there was a vibe he gave off that didn't sit right with Megan, something about his shallow eyes and the flat tone of his voice. It wasn't until Megan found her mother weeping over the kitchen sink that her intuition was proven right.

Deborah confessed to her daughter she found romantic texts and active dating profiles on Scott's phone. When she confronted him, Scott proceeded to gaslight her, blaming her for depriving him of his privacy and being an unsatisfactory partner. He called her delusional, paranoid, and not ready for a relationship with the kind of baggage she held onto. There was no remorse, no apology. Deborah promptly threw him out of the house. Scott obliged, but although the breakup was swift, Megan's mother was worse for wear as she'd let another man walk all over her, leaving her with stinging insults and an emotional punch to the gut. Luckily, Megan never saw Scott or any of her mother's other boyfriends hit her. If she ever caught wind of that, especially now that she was older, she wouldn't hesitate to take the man's life. No question about it.

From a young age, Megan knew she had to watch her back when it came to the opposite sex. At any given moment, they could get aggressive or turn around and cheat on you with someone else. Even at the age of eighteen, Megan knew men were never to be trusted.

To an outsider, one would think Megan wanted nothing to do with men by any means. It would make sense, after all. If a child is brought up with a negative connotation of men, how would they ever form a proper relationship with one? But that wasn't the case at all. Megan has had several boyfriends in her life. She's been in love and has had loving, genuine experiences with the guys she's met, whether from her senior class or her job waiting tables at the diner not far from her house. Sure, there was a lot of nonsense she had to go through to find them, but they made themselves known nonetheless.

In between the immature older men and overly flirty dudes eating out at the diner, Megan found a respectful date. Even now, as Megan was trapped behind the sealed door of Room 222 inside Shaded Grove Mental Hospital, she had a boyfriend back home. Gage Johnson, a twenty-one-year-old landscaper who had more tattoos than hairs on his head. It was too bad *he* didn't attend the out-of-town haunted house birthday trip. If Gage was stuck in the old hospital, he would've been able to break down the front gate with his bare hands. At least Megan thought so. She wondered how Gage would've reacted seeing Todd or the shaking old man who exploded into a dirty floating cloud.

As for believing in ghosts, demons, and otherworldly entities like her younger sister, Megan wasn't on board. She thought all that stuff was old folklore, nothing more than spooky traditions and stories that somehow made it through the generations. Sure, the idea of someone's soul manifesting into a pale phantom and roaming the earth was creepy, but it couldn't be any scarier than what living, fleshy human beings were capable of. Murder. Rape. Violence against children and innocent people. Who needed ghosts and ghoulies when you had twisted acts like those? Megan often wondered why her sister even entertained the idea of the paranormal.

Nevertheless, Megan loved her sister with her whole heart. Although Dianne got on her nerves with her different phases and interests over the years, Megan would always go out of her way to spend time with her and fulfill any request she had, even if it was something totally opposite of what Megan believed in. Just like the Ashford House ghost tour in the middle of nowhere.

As rooted in logic as she was, Megan was out of ways to rationalize the night's horrors playing out in Shaded Grove. At first, she could see an old, demented woman wandering away from her nursing home or escaping her family's house. She could see how the woman could get triggered and throw a fit, causing a car accident. Things got more complicated than that; what about Todd, the mysterious security guard that disappeared? Megan could see how he left the scene and dropped his flashlight on the concrete path outside. Maybe there was another emergency, and he just forgot all about the poor sisters in the rain. *All right, fair enough.*

Trickier still, what about Gerald Swaggart? He appeared out of nowhere and disappeared into dust right before Megan's eyes. Although she initially theorized about this being some elaborate prank show, even wondering if Dianne was in on it, she could not explain how that happened. There was no sign of the old man after he burst. Unless there was a trap door or something, there was no indication that it was special effects. It terrified Megan and made her question everything. If there really were ghosts here in this abandoned mental ward, could the spirits that supposedly roamed the Ashford House be real, too?

Megan didn't know, and she definitely didn't know how she would get out of Room 222. She worried about her sister exploring the wing and couldn't think straight about her own escape. It also wasn't helping that the room she was in was filthy and stained all up and down the walls with black rot and disgusting graffiti displaying demon heads with bloodied mouths half crumbled away by decay. Somehow, this room got the short end of the stick compared to the room across the hall. At least there was a bed in 221. In 222, there was just a pile of destroyed boxes, springs, and pieces of wood that were too jagged and rotten to touch, nothing of any use to smash the window on the door or the window with the bars that faced outside.

All Megan could do for the moment was wait and let her thoughts stew in her mind and try to push away the waves of claustrophobia that relentlessly kept creeping closer, ready to consume her any second. It was like being in prison, stuck between four walls with nothing but yourself and the fear of the uncertainty of your future.

She walked over to the window that faced outside. The rain was slower, but the droplets still covered the glass. Megan made out the darkened trees just beyond the barbed wire fence. If she could get the window open, she believed she could jump and make it over the wire top. She'd probably break her legs in the process, but she'd be on the other side. Wouldn't it be better to be trapped out in the wilderness than confined in a smelly, disgusting mental ward that's been trashed ten times over? Legs or no legs?

The mental hospital broke her down. All Megan wanted was fresh air. It felt like lifetimes had passed since she could breathe. The suffocation drove her mad.

Faint thunder rumbled in the distance as the rain slowly pulled away. A lightning strike flashed somewhere beyond the dead trees. Megan saw her pale face reflecting in the dark window.

Not only hers but another behind her.

Chapter 7

The Ashford House

For a girl like Dianne, going to a haunted house was the equivalent of a child going to Toys R Us to pick out anything they wanted. Half the fun was the anticipation, but instead of getting excited about running up and down the isles to find the perfect toy, Dianne looked forward to seeing, hearing, or feeling the presence of a spirit. Just *standing* inside a house with a ghost story got her toes wiggling and her energies vibrating.

With Dianne's sixteenth birthday around the corner, she wanted to find a new, old house to tour. The problem was the girl had already visited all of the local joints. She went on all of the Gettysburg tours and the various fringe places outside the city, so she had to search online to find any outside the county but not too far for Megan to drive.

Pickings were slim outside of the Civil War region of the state, but Dianne came across a place called the Ashford House, a house built in the late 1800s that sat in a small town called Shaded Grove, Pennsylvania. Dianne had never heard of Shaded Grove, but she was intrigued by the story posted on the tour's website.

In classic haunted house fashion, the history of the place revolved around a crazed mother who murdered her husband, children, and ultimately herself via hanging. Sure, it wasn't the most original setup for a ghost tour, but it was the most gruesome backstory Dianne had encountered so far. She usually found herself in old homes where there was maybe one murder or a freak accident where a clock fell and crushed someone's head. In the case of the Civil War tours, there was always the spirit of a soldier or an innocent person struck by a stray bullet that came through the wall. This place provided familial bloodshed with children involved, something a little grittier for Dianne.

It may have been a lengthy drive, but the sisters made it with enough time to get a bite to eat at a local restaurant called Troy's Place in the central part of Shaded Grove, which only consisted of a general store, a fire department, and an auto shop, none of which looked like they moved on from the mid-1990s. The whole feel of the town was vintage, frozen in time.

When they made it to the Ashford House, there were only a few other cars parked alongside the road. Although the tour itself didn't cost much to get in--ten bucks per person--the distance was probably too much for a lot of people. Halloween had already passed, so folks weren't itching to get their spooky fix, not that they'd want to come here anyway. For Pennsylvanians, the main attractions for the fall season were Field of Screams or Jason's Woods, places where people dressed up as killer clowns and chain-saw-wielding maniacs who popped out of professionally designed rides and houses. Fun stuff, sure, but Dianne liked the true stories. The authentic lore.

That's where the Ashford House came in.

Dianne and Megan parked the Ford behind one of the

other cars and walked along the side of the road until they came to a wooden sign with ASHFORD HOUSE painted on it in white. An arrow pointed to the right just below.

A long field led to a house. It stood all by its lonesome as another field sat beside it. A sea of trees beyond. There were no other houses in sight as the Ashford House stood isolated on the small, rural piece of land, like aliens had dropped the property down from the sky.

The other tour participants were up ahead, walking along the stone path that led to the house. A cool breeze came across the moderately warm late-autumn day as the sisters stepped on the trail themselves.

"Here we go," Megan said as she zipped up her leather jacket. "Are you scared yet?"

"Not yet, but I hope I will be," Dianne replied.

"Me, too. Coming out this far, I *better* see a ghost."

"What if you do, though? Will your whole life be changed?"

"Honestly, it would. If I have a real experience, like, it's one hundred percent a paranormal encounter that isn't a goof, I think it would."

"Oh yeah?"

"Yeah, but the problem is, these places always have a gimmick. How much you wanna bet that they have speakers in the walls to make things more creepy?"

Dianne shook her head. "You're no fun."

"I'm just keeping it real! I haven't seen anything during any of these ghost tours I've been on. It's always the same stuff. Orbs. Oh, did you hear that? I could've sworn I saw something!" Megan was getting animated, already starting to annoy her sister.

"Well, don't ruin it for the rest of us," Dianne said,

nudging her sister on the elbow. "Some of us actually believe."

"Look, I came all the way out here. I wanna see a *ghost*, not another dust particle on my phone."

"If you talk like that, you're probably not gonna see one," Dianne said. She was about ready to wrestle with her sister right there in the field, they were like brothers in that regard, fighting with one another in ways only siblings knew, but they were too close to the house and other visitors to get physical.

Up close, the Ashford House was worn, weathered by the elements and time. It was made of wood and was wide with two floors. Tiny windows went up to the roof. A stained chimney stood in the middle. Below, old steps went up to a porch that wrapped around the front. The wood had a greenish tinge to it, and the white paint that covered the door and railings was chipped, exposing a grayed surface beneath.

Dianne got her phone out to start taking photographs, hoping to snap a picture of a ghost staring back at her from one of the windows or an apparition just beside the door. She couldn't contain her excitement even before the tour started.

Chapter 8

The Nurse's Station

Dianne wanted to run, but the multiple holes in the floor made her move with cautious steps as she ventured down the opposite end of the second-floor hallway.

Some of the doors to the other patient rooms were inaccessible as holes opened before them. Others were locked tight. The rooms that Dianne *could* enter held nothing but more depressing decay and useless pieces of trash. She needed a key or a tool that she could leverage between the door and doorframe of Room 222.

Dust particles danced in Dianne's light as she moved to the center of the hallway, where two dead elevators stood to her right and a counter connected to the wall on her left. Broken wooden chairs lay beneath it. Above, a window looked out to the other buildings outside. Dianne saw someone walking on the other side of the grounds, toward the two smaller buildings beyond the Administration Building. Dianne thought the shape of the figure looked like Todd or, rather, the ghost of Todd.

As far as Dianne was concerned, no one in Shaded

Grove Mental Hospital was alive. She had to treat every encounter as a paranormal one, approaching whatever spirit she met with an open mind and as much kindness as she could muster. That's what she learned from other ghost enthusiasts. Then again, considering her good behavior toward Todd and Gerald, why was she attacked in the stairwell?

Dianne wondered if she should go outside and search for Todd, maybe convince him to help her open the door. He probably had access to every room in the joint. But now that she thought about it, not only could there be a key down at the nurse's station, but there might also be one back in the guard post. Dianne might not have to interact with Todd again, if it was Todd out there, after all. It'd be faster to keep at it alone.

With these ideas floating around her panicked mind, Dianne kept moving, walking down the hall, checking the doors of the rooms for anything inside to help make her mission end sooner than later.

One of the doors had a placard that was half-ripped away, leaving only the word WASH. No holes blocked the entrance, so Dianne approached it, finding it unlocked. Not wanting to leave any stone unturned, she pulled on the handle and opened the door to reveal multiple bathtubs and shower curtains in a white-tiled room with large red splats of stains. Brown, rusty material covered the walls, too.

As she stood in the doorway and took in the smashed porcelain and continued decay, Dianne heard a ding sound from behind her. She leaned back into the hallway and pointed her flashlight to see a white light blinking above where the elevators were, the same ones that were dark and inoperable a moment ago. There were no other signs of the power being back on, just the dinging and ball-shaped bulb going off.

Dianne went into the washroom before the sound of the rickety elevator rising and opening finished. After she shut the door, footsteps echoed in the hall. Squeaky wheels. A woman's voice. A man groaning and moaning. All the sounds merged together, coming closer.

"We're almost there, Franklin. Just take some deep breaths," the woman in the hall said.

Franklin groaned some more in response. His voice sounded aged and gravely, like he was a lifetime smoker of unfiltered cigarettes.

Ducking below the window on the door, Dianne clicked off her flashlight. She held her breath, trying not to make a single noise as the sounds of the two people passed by in the hall.

"I'm gonna make sure you're tucked in tight, all right? I'll give you something to help you sleep," the woman said, her voice starting to sound a little farther away, along with the gurgling noise of the man.

Dianne kept silent for a few more moments. After she felt comfortable enough, she clicked on her flashlight and slowly stood herself back up to peek out the window. It was too dark to see, so she'd have to open the door a crack and aim her light into the hall to see if the coast was truly clear.

When she eased the washroom door open and let the hinges whine for a second, Dianne covered the face of her flashlight, only allowing some of the orangish light out into the hall. Doing so, she saw the back of a nurse entering one of the patient rooms up ahead. Dianne had to lean back into the washroom for a split second so she wouldn't be noticed. Then, after waiting for half a minute, she stuck her head back out, seeing no signs of anyone else around.

The sound of the man groaning returned, making Dianne panic and shut off her light again. This made it hard for her to maneuver the hall as the holes were barely noticeable in the darkness. She already moved slowly toward the patient's room, but now she had to walk with such slowness that Dianne was just about standing still in the hallway. So, in order to stay on track, Dianne got down on all fours and started to crawl, patting around the slimy, grimy floor to feel for any holes.

"Can you stand for me?" the nurse said from the room up ahead.

There was movement. Clicking noises. Footsteps. A burp.

"There you go. You're doing a great job, Franklin."

Dianne kept her slow crawl up, maneuvering around the holes, when she felt the tiles turn to a concrete-like material with jagged edges. She tried to breathe easy and not too loud.

"Let's get you into bed now. Easy does it. I've got you."

The voice was closer now. Dianne heard the nurse talking from the other side of the wall. She heard bedsprings being pressed down. Mumbling. Groaning. The sound of sheets being whipped out to lay over a mattress.

"Ok, I'm going to get you all hooked up now so you can get a good night's rest," the nurse said. "Is there anything else I can get you tonight, Franklin?"

Dianne felt the bottom of the doorframe. Her hand wrapped around it until she got on her feet and crouched beneath the doorway. She moved over to the side and eased her head toward the window to spy on the scene inside.

Just like how the light above the elevator doors worked, a small desk lamp sat alight on the end table beside Franklin's bed in the center of the room. It was the only light source in the whole space, but it gave off enough glow to show Dianne that the nurse and Franklin were among the usual filth. Gerald didn't mind it before, and neither did these two. They seemed unaffected by the surrounding rust and graffiti.

But that's how it went with spirits. From what Dianne gathered from her previous research, the souls of those unable to move on from the physical realm are doomed to repeat the activities they performed before their passing. These nurses and patients may be dead, but since they haven't ascended anywhere, they'll just continue to go about their daily routines despite what happened to the environment they used to live in. That's why they're not alarmed at their new, hellish surroundings. To them, they only see what was in the past. Instead of being inside of a room that's wrecked beyond proper living conditions, they're seeing the place how it once was back in the day. They think nothing's out of the ordinary, that the bed is not torn to shreds, that the walls are not spray painted, and that there are no holes to be found on the floors. Dianne and Megan see it all because they're in the present time, but they're the only ones.

"You did a very good job today," the nurse said. Her back faced Dianne as she worked with the IV bag beside the bed. There was a dark liquid inside, nothing that Dianne could identify. Usually, in hospitals, there was blood or a clear substance. Whatever this was, it looked too dangerous to be put into someone's veins. "I think you're gonna have a nice rest tonight."

Franklin muttered something. All Dianne saw of him was his patchy beard and the top of his hospital gown poking out of the top of the stained bedsheets.

"If you need anything, just call for me. I'll be right up,

ok?" the nurse said. "If I'm on break, I'll have Claire come up to take care of you. You like Claire, don't you? She's a sweet girl."

Claire..., Dianne thought. *The nurse Gerald was looking for.*

Franklin gave a few more groans for the evening as the nurse finished with the IV. She flicked off the end table lamp and turned from the bed. Dianne moved her head out of the window before backing away from the door, retreating into the dark corner of the hall. While maneuvering without the flashlight turned on, her heel met a small hole in the floor, causing Dianne to trip and fall backward onto her butt. Luckily, she didn't land in another, bigger hole.

The door to Franklin's room opened. With her eyes slightly adjusted to the darkness, Dianne saw the nurse step out and spin around to lock the door with a little key that slipped into the pocket of her uniform, a vintage apron atop a blue shirt. She also donned a white hat, white shoes, and long socks that disappeared into her skirt.

For a brief moment, the nurse stopped and stared in Dianne's direction, and their eyes met in the darkness. They were like two statues. One living. One dead. Dianne wasn't sure if the nurse was really looking *at* her, or beyond her, or what, but she was frozen in fear, terrified of what the spirit would do to her as she sat defenseless on the floor of the hallway.

The nurse didn't speak as she turned away from Dianne, seeming not to have noticed the scared fifteen-year-old girl in the corner after all. She casually walked down the hall toward the elevator doors, floating above any holes that were in her way. In her world, the floor was intact, posing no danger of tripping and falling through it.

Dianne started to crawl behind the nurse, making sure not to move too fast, or make any loud noises as she felt for any openings in the floor again. The nurse walked at a regular pace, only stopping to look into the window of one of the other rooms. She didn't go inside any of them.

Up ahead, the white light above the elevators reignited. The nurse approached them and pressed the button between them. Doing so brought back the ding sound and caused the old metal door to open on its loose track.

There was no way Dianne was going to get inside either of the elevators. She may not be the smartest girl in the world, but she wasn't dumb enough to think that getting into a sealed box inside Shaded Grove would be a good idea. The ride may go up and down for the nurse, but the moment Dianne stepped inside, there was no doubt it would either trap her behind the metal doors or take her to a floor that didn't exist on this plane. Either way, Dianne wasn't interested in tailing the woman like that. If she was going to return to the first floor, she'd either jump down the stairwell at the end of the hall or simply fall through one of the holes. Either option was miles better than taking a ride on the elevators.

The elevator descended before Dianne heard the ding down below. She saw the faint white glow of the elevator light from one of the holes. Dianne angled her neck around so she could see the nurse step out and walk to the nurse's station directly across, placing her key down on the desk. Dianne watched her open a drawer and pull something out of it.

The nurse hummed to herself as she scribbled something down. Another item came from the drawer, and the nurse gave it a tap on the desk before she turned and exited Wing A while she continued singing her little tune.

A lock clicked open. A door creaked wide and shut. Everything fell silent, and the lights above the elevators vanished, bringing back the total darkness. Dianne waited for a second, listening for any sounds in the blackness, any indication of not being alone. When none came, she flicked her flashlight back on and thought about the best way to get back downstairs. The memory of the ghost army pulling on her dangling feet returned to her.

I have to go quick, she thought. *Get the key and get out.* 222. 222. Dianne repeated the number so she could stay focused. *Room 222. That key has to be down there.* 222.

Behind her, just down the hall from where she crawled a moment ago, Dianne heard a loud groan, the familiar whining of Franklin. She shined her light, finding no sign of the man standing there, however, Dianne wasn't going to wait around to see if Franklin would make himself known. So, in an effort to save time and an inevitable scream, Dianne found the widest hole next to her and lowered herself down.

The distance between the two floors wasn't as far as Dianne thought. There was only about five feet below Dianne's dangling sneakers as she let her body drop to the tiled floor. Her knees bent, and she rolled a little to the side, getting her hands dirty from slapping against a soaked newspaper. Dianne quickly got up and wiped her hands on her jeans, not that they were that clean, either. Her whole outfit, her jacket, pants, and shoes, was filthy with dirt and rain. She needed a hot shower when this was all over. A deep scrub down from head to toe.

After checking down both sides of the first-floor hall with her flashlight, Dianne went to the U-shaped nurse's station that stood before the main entrance's double doors. She stepped around the counter of the station to discover the lower desk was littered with papers. When Dianne's light moved among them, she saw they were medical records, half-pieces of tan paper with faded typewriter-style font. Names of men and women admitted to Shaded Grove for their mental illnesses. Depression. Anxiety. Paranoia. But one that caught Dianne's eye was a woman, Margaret L. Rose, who was admitted in June of 1951 on account of CONSTANT LAUGHTER. FAILURE TO CEASE HYSTERICAL BEHAVIOR. LUNATIC. Beneath that was mention of electroshock therapy. Sedation.

As interesting and horrifying as the old medical record was, Dianne had to turn her attention to the drawers. She positioned herself where she saw the nurse a moment ago.

There were three metal drawers on the side of the station. All of them were locked tight. Dianne gave another glance around to see if the coast was clear before she started to really pull on the handles, giving them a good yank. She heard jingling and jangling sounds coming from inside the top drawer as she struggled, but no matter how hard she pulled, the drawers wouldn't budge. Dianne grew irritated.

In the corner of the desk, beneath the top counter of the station, was a lined piece of paper on a clipboard. Dianne remembered seeing the nurse writing in the dark, so she shined her flashlight over it as she brought the clipboard toward her.

It appeared to be a check-in, check-out sheet with names of the doctors and nurses written in the left column, while times and signatures were in the columns on the right. At a glance, Dianne saw the signature of Nurse Claire Silva. Not far from it, Nurse Alyssa Grantham, who was at the bottom of the chart, signed out at 4:00 AM.

Dianne tried the drawer again, giving the handle a firm tug. It still didn't budge. Then, she remembered the key in her pocket. She dug it out and tried to slide it into the lock, but it wouldn't go in, not even a little bit. Dianne wanted to swear in her despair, scream out into the darkness, but she didn't allow herself to break down. Not yet.

As she stood for a moment, eyeing over the spread contents of the desk, breathing heavy, stress-filled breaths, Dianne noticed another familiar name poking out of the stack of medical records. She shined her light above it and pinched the half-sheet out of the stack. It read:

No. 119

Name: SWAGGART, GERALD M.

Religion: CATHOLIC

Residence: 208 EAST 26TH ST, MORNINGSIDE, PA

Date of Admission: MAR. 21, 1953

Diagnosis: UNRULY CONFUSION AND EXPLO-SIVE AGITATION. ANXIETY.

Treatment Notes: RESPONDS REASONABLY WELL TO HYDROTHERAPY (WARM)

"Well," Dianne said to herself. "That explains it." She thought back to how the man went for her sister, attacking her in the hall before he turned into ashes, a cloud of dust. Dianne shook her head before she put the record down beside yet another name that she had recently discovered.

No. 153

Name: HALE, FRANKLIN J.

Religion: PROTESTANT

Residence: 45 RED MILL ROAD, HUNTINGTON, PA

Date of Admission: OCT. 10, 1955

Diagnosis: MENTAL RETARDATION

Treatment Notes: ELECTROSHOCK INEFFEC-TIVE. FEVER THERAPY WITHOUT MUCH

IMPROVEMENT. MAY REQUIRE INSULIN FOR FUTURE TREATMENTS AND REPLACEMENT IN BASEMENT. WILL WATCH.

Dianne felt sick. Whatever "fever therapy" was, she didn't want to know. It sounded cruel and inhumane.

What would they be using insulin for?

There would be time for further research later. Right now, Dianne had to get access to the drawer that she believed held the key to Room 222, or at least the key to getting her closer to freeing her sister. Dianne was going to have to go outside to follow Nurse Grantham and somehow get the key from her pocket, or whatever access she had to the drawers in Wing A, and who knows what would be waiting back out there, where Nurse Grantham was off to, or if she was even still around. For all Dianne knew, the nurse could have vanished already, faded back into the dimension she came from for the moment. She would have to find her or hope to God there was another key in Todd's guard post.

Dianne gave the nurse's station another quick scan, finding no other keys or tools she could use among the scattered notes and miscellaneous office supplies. There were more medical records of patients with severe mental illnesses and controversial treatments, but Dianne didn't have time to comb through them as she turned from the desk and approached the main entrance's double doors.

The windows were dark as the sun was yet to poke its head out over the horizon. Dianne clicked off her flashlight before she gently pushed open the right door and stepped out into the blackness of the hospital grounds again.

Chapter 9

The Laughter in the Dark

There was no one in the room, at least not that Megan could see. Despite the face staring back at her from the reflection in the window, Megan found herself still trapped all by herself in Room 222. Cold. Tired. Afraid. Helpless. *Hope*less. It wasn't that she had no confidence in her sister to get her out, it was that Shaded Grove was unpredictable, unexplainable in its actions. Figures coming and going. Strong, invisible forces. Faces appearing out of the blackness. Megan hoped that wherever Dianne was, she was safe and out of harm's way from the entities that lurked the halls and grounds of the old hospital.

In her panic and worry, Megan returned to the door, where she kicked and punched against the wood. She almost struck her elbow against the door but quickly remembered the pain she felt whenever she bent it in a certain way. Megan meant to look at her arm to check for the inevitable bruises, but she had no desire to face any more issues. Her imprisonment was enough. If her arm was broken, she didn't want to know just yet. Once she and

Dianne escaped from Shaded Grove, her body would get the proper treatment it deserved.

Like everything else, the bathroom of Room 222 was trashed and disgusting. Megan could only take one step inside until she had to turn and cover her nose from the putrid scent of the unflushed past. The odors of ancient feces and urine were ingrained into the walls and floor. She wanted to see if there was anything inside that she could use, but nothing looked helpful from where she stood in the doorway shining her flashlight.

"Jesus Christ," she said with her hand over her nose, her fingers pinching her nostrils tight. "Get me out of this place!"

There was no space to sit in the room, no wall that was clean enough to lean against. The corners were filthy. The floor was rubble. Megan had to stand around or pace as she waited for her sister to return.

Was Megan a believer now? Was she shown enough paranormal and unexplainable evidence to finally put her pride to the side and agree with Dianne that spirits did, in fact, exist on this plane? Probably, but this was no time to bask in any great revelations. Then again, maybe that was the whole message behind the events of the night. If the entire disaster was a ruse and nothing more than a prank to get Megan to admit she was wrong, maybe that was the real key to getting out of the hospital. Perhaps if Megan came out and said she knew ghosts and spirits were real and that she'd take energies more seriously, the cameras would show themselves, and the producers of this hellish ride would be exposed once and for all.

What did she have to lose?

"All right," Megan said as she stood in the center of the room. "You got me! I give up!" She raised her voice. "I believe in ghosts, ok? I'm scared! You win. Whoever you are, you win! I don't want to do this anymore!"

Megan looked around the room, checking for any movement. When nothing happened, she went back over to the door to continue her great surrender, thinking that she'd be better heard with her face up against the glass of the window.

"I don't want to be stuck in here anymore! I'm sorry, ok? Whatever you want me to say, I'll say! There's no reason to continue doing this! I'm scared and ready to go home! Please! I believe! I believe!"

There was a pause as Megan caught her breath. All the talking made her winded, so she rested her head against the wood of the door. She didn't have a lot of energy to be so loud.

Just then, as Megan was about to start again, a faint sound of laughter came up from the hall outside. It made Megan snap her head back from the door. Her eyes widened as she stood with total stillness, listening to the laughter that sounded like it came from a woman somewhere in the distance.

"Hello?" Megan said. "Who's out there?"

There was silence, followed by the laughter returning, slightly louder now.

"Dianne, is that you?" Megan punched the door. "Dianne, if that's you—"

The laughter grew closer. Megan could hear it wasn't an old, gravelly voice but a younger one. Youthful.

"Hello?" Megan continued to slap on the wood. "If someone's out there, come get me out of this room! I swear, Dianne, if this is some kind of a sick joke, I'm gonna kill you! I swear to God!"

There was nothing pleasant about the female laugh

from the hall, but the worst, most frightening part, was that it was constant. There would be short pauses, but the laughs were a continuous stream of HA-HA-HAs, like it was the Joker from Batman. Maniacal. Evil. The exact opposite of how you want to sound when you find something humorous, and there was certainly nothing humorous or remotely funny about Shaded Grove.

"Who are you?" Megan asked. "What do you want from me?"

The laughter continued, growing in volume by the second. Soon, it started to sound bigger than a human's voice, like it was coming from something far greater in size.

Although the dust from Gerald's vanishing was almost all settled, Megan still couldn't see much out of the window. There was so much darkness staring back at her that she would probably miss it if someone walked by the door. She was only able to see Dianne before because Dianne had her face pressing against it. Even then, Megan had to look hard to make out that it was her.

"Ok, I get it!" Megan shouted, desperate for peace. "I hear you!"

The laughter stopped in mid-laugh. Megan waited, listening until pounding came from the other side of the door. The wood rocked in the frame as the sound of multiple fists came crashing from the other side. Megan screamed and jumped back, almost tripping on a piece of cardboard on the floor. She had her hands over her ears as the banging was so loud. Not only that, but the laughter returned, as maniacal and unsettling as ever.

HA-HA-HA-HA-HA!
Bang, bang, bang!
HA-HA-HA-HA-HA!
Bang, bang, bang!

Megan wanted to throw her flashlight at the door to cease the unending sounds but stopped herself as she realized it would extinguish the only bit of light she had.

"Stop it! Shut up!" she screamed, making her voice crack. Her throat burned. "Get out of here!"

And so, it did. The pounding subsided. The laughter stopped again. There was silence. No noise came from outside at all. Surprisingly, Megan's shouting demand brought the commotion from beyond the door to a halt.

"Thank you," Megan sighed. "Jesus... Whoever's out there, please just let me out. I told you, I'm over all this. It's not funny anymore. I'm so tired..."

No response. No sound of the door opening. No key in the lock. Nothing.

With hesitant steps, Megan returned to the door, trying to see if there was anyone outside that she could see, but only the blackness remained through the glass. She tried the handle before placing her head against the wood, pressing her ear to listen for any whispers or people talking on the other side. There was nothing at first.

Megan stood still in her focus when she heard fast footsteps on the tiles outside. They were followed by a single slap against the other side of the window. Megan jumped back again, seeing a pale hand pressing hard against the glass. It disappeared into the dark. The same maniacal laughter floated down the hallway, becoming fainter as it continued to echo.

All Megan could do now was scream.

Chapter 10

The Ashford House Part II

Although there weren't a lot of ghost tour-goers at the Ashford House on the late November evening, there wasn't a whole lot of space inside the foyer. There was a red-haired guy with his blonde girlfriend, a tatted-up biker dude with his equally inked wife, a single nerdy man with huge glasses and a video camera, and, of course, the Willis sisters.

The seven of them stood close together inside the entrance of the chilly house as Michelle, the heavyset tour guide who donned a long-sleeved shirt with an outline of the house itself, stood before the staircase as she detailed the horrific story that cursed the house forever.

"So, this house was built in 1867, not long after the Civil War ended." She spoke with a slight rural twang. A backwoods Pittsburghian tone. "However, the town of Shaded Grove was never involved with the war directly, there were never any battles fought around these parts, and as far as the records go back, there were less than ten men who were drafted from this part of the county. In those days, the Grove was even more unknown than it is now."

Michelle chuckled, making her rosy cheeks push against her eyes. "Not that that was such a bad thing, it just meant that the community here was very small, and everyone knew one another. That's why the tale of the Ashfords has stuck around for so long. When the tragic death of the entire family hit in the late-1800s, everyone around here knew about it and kept a good record of the aftermath, along with the several theories that formed. It's stayed with the town ever since. Of course, there are other things Shaded Grove is known for, but that's for a whole other tour someday." She chuckled again and shook her head. "You just never know what's gonna happen in these parts."

"Anywho, let me just go over a few things before we get into the meat of it. You're all allowed to take all the photos and videos you'd like. We just ask that you keep your technology set on silent if you could. We wanna make sure we have as much silence as we can so we can keep an ear out for any of the spirits that roam this place. You don't wanna miss a thing while you're here, believe me. We've had all sorts of things happen during these tours. Voices. Whispering from the rooms upstairs. Footsteps. And you can best believe the kinds of photos people take here are incredible. If you haven't already, check out our Facebook page. We have all kinds of great videos and pictures from the tours. Really compelling stuff. I saw some of you taking photos outside. One time we had a woman go back and look over her pictures, and she saw a full outline of a person standing in the window of the master bedroom. Some say it was Nancy Ashford herself, keeping an eye on the visitors."

The group nodded to one another. Everyone seemed excited to hopefully capture a hard piece of evidence like that themselves, Dianne included. She looked over at her sister, who was taking in the wooden-slat walls, the sepia-toned photographs, and the overall darkened atmosphere of the 19th-century house.

"If any of you have a question, or want to add something to what I'm sayin', just raise your hand or yell out 'Michelle!' I am always surprised at what new knowledge I can get from the folks that come out to the tour."

"Won't be gettin' a whole lot from us," the leather-clad biker man said with a smile. "We just came through on a ride and thought we'd stop in for something spooky. Never been to Shaded Grove before."

Michelle laughed. "I'm glad you could join us. I know a lot of folks find this place by surprise, whether on a road trip or through the internet. It's a nice, tucked-away town with a lot of history. I hope you'll tell your friends all about it."

"Only if we see some ghosts!" the biker man said before he went into a loud smoker's laugh.

A big smile came across Michelle's face. "I'm sure you'll at least *feel* something here. Everyone has an experience, whether it's during or after the tour. There's a spiritual energy that will attach to you when you're in the house long enough. Now, let's first begin with..."

Michelle went on to detail the history of the Ashfords and how they all perished in the horrific murder-suicide brought out by mother and wife, Nancy Ashford, the typical brown-haired American housewife who kept the children well-fed and dressed while she also tended to the house. She went to church, helped fellow members of the community, and was as non-threatening as people came. As others had stated in the past, Nancy was a shy woman who was never known to be angered or overly animated. She was sociable and well-spoken. God-fearing. Pretty. Healthy. A good wife to her husband, Ethan, a farmer, and a proper mother to her three children, Jack, John, and Lily.

To everyone living in Shaded Grove back in the late-1800s, there was nothing out of the ordinary about the woman. That was, until one evening, she decided to kill her entire family before taking her own life, bringing about the most gruesome murder the town had ever seen.

Michelle lifted her arms in the air and said, "Now, I don't want to freak any of you out right off the bat, although that *is* kind of my job." She chuckled. "But where you're all standing in the parlor is where Nancy took her husband's life. When Ethan came back inside from a long day's work in the fields outside, Nancy was waiting right on these steps, holding a bloody knife behind her back, the same exact knife she used to kill her daughter and two sons."

The red-haired guy looked down at the hardwood floor as if he was about to see a bloodstain staring back at him. The guy with the giant glasses recorded with his camera.

"Ethan was concerned when he came home to find Nancy wearing a blood-covered dress on the landing. When he approached her and reached out for her, she revealed the knife and began to stab her husband in the chest a reported seventeen times."

"Holy smokes," the biker woman said.

"Holy smokes is right," Michelle said. "Nancy kept driving the knife deep into her husband's chest until his body collapsed and bled out on the floor on which you are all standing on right now. Of course, after many cleanings and years gone by, you cannot see the full spots today. However, it's said, in the right light, you can see just tiny, tiny, dried droplets of Ethan Ashford's blood on the wood as the attack was so deep into his flesh, the blood soaked into the wood boards."

"That's spooky," the blonde girl said to herself. She held her boyfriend's hand tighter.

"Wild stuff," Megan whispered to her sister.

Dianne only nodded. She knew if she acknowledged Megan too much, Megan would be making comments for the whole tour. Dianne didn't want to risk having Michelle or any of the other visitors overhearing a smartass remark.

"But you'll have to pay close attention, though," Michelle said. "The tour of the Ashford House is all over the place just because of the fact that the murders went on all throughout here. We're really telling the story backward, minus Nancy's suicide, which happened upstairs. It's kind of like a sandwich. The two pieces of bread are Ethan and Nancy's deaths, with the children in the middle. Does that make sense?"

Everyone nodded.

"Great, so let's next move on to the kitchen," Michelle said, motioning to the right, the group's left. "Keep in mind, since Nancy had no regard for the mess she made, the blood trailed throughout the house. No matter where you're standing, you're going to be on top of where the family's blood fell. A piece of the Ashfords will be at every turn. There's no 'safe space,' so to speak. That's why you might find an orb or figure in any photos you take in any of the rooms. Sounds. Presences. Be mindful that you're walking on very active ground and that you should take it very seriously."

Dianne knew Megan was rolling her eyes, but she didn't pay her any mind for the moment. Instead, she focused on her surroundings, the small kitchen with a tiny iron stove by the window. A couple of cabinets on the wall. Blackened pots and pans hanging in the corner. The circular table that sat in the middle of it all.

The group squeezed in the even tighter space, snapping

pictures with their phones as they all listened to Michelle continuing the story of the family's demise.

"Lily was the daughter of the family, a little girl by the age of four. She looked just like her mother with the same long, brown hair. Brown eyes. Unfortunately, Lily was the first family member to be murdered when Nancy snapped and grabbed the biggest knife she could find in here."

"There were many different theories as to why Nancy suddenly decided to commit the most evil act of all. Some said she was possessed by the devil after losing her faith in the church, while some suggested that she dabbled in the dark arts. Rituals, stuff like that. Other folks believed that there was something wrong with the well water, and that led to a disease in her brain, degenerating all logical and moral thought. Kind of like a parasite that infected her body."

"We could spend all night trying to figure out what exactly set Nancy Ashford off, but we'd probably talk in circles. As time goes on, we get farther from the true origins of the murders. However, we will be trying to contact the Ashfords a little later on to see if we can get any clues, to see what really compelled her to do what she did."

"Either way, no matter what theory you believe in, Nancy came into the kitchen, grabbed the steak knife from the drawer, and called little Lily to come to her." Michelle pointed back toward the living room across the foyer. "Lily was playing with her toys at the time and, of course, listened to her mother's every command, so she dropped everything and rushed over to the kitchen, unaware that her mother was about to kill her."

"Jeez," the blond-haired girl said, shifting her body nervously.

"Right here in the kitchen is where Nancy did her

deed," Michelle said. "There was blood everywhere. All over the floor. The table. The cabinets. Everywhere. Luckily, Lily didn't suffer long, not like Ethan Ashford did. Nancy was done with her rather quickly before she went upstairs to take care of her twin boys."

"Sounds like a real demon woman if you ask me," the biker man said as his eyebrows curled. He was like a detective investigating a crime scene in the way he examined the table.

"Before we move to the rooms upstairs, I'll give you all some time to look around and get a feel for the atmosphere," Michelle said. "Feel free to go back into the foyer and living area as well. There's a lot of energy around here that won't be going anywhere anytime soon."

The group started to break away a bit. The biker couple looked around the kitchen while the guy with glasses filmed every object. Megan and Dianne went back to the foyer with the red-haired guy and his girlfriend as the four of them went to explore the living room, where dust covered the rocking chairs and the ashy fireplace lay empty. Above it, the mantel held aged black and white photographs of a baby, children, and what must've been Nancy and Ethan Ashford, decked head to toe in vintage wear of the late 19th century: a ruffled dress and a thick three-piece suit.

Dianne took some more photos on her phone before she opened the voice recorder app. She held the phone out about two feet from her chest.

"What are you doing?" Megan asked as she gave her sister a strange look.

"I'm recording to see if I pick up any strange voices," Dianne replied. "Ever heard of EVP?"

Megan shook her head and smiled. She turned from her sister and started looking around the living room herself, taking in the faded carpet, the tables with silver candle holders. "How are you going to catch voices if we're talking? How would you hear them?"

"It's in-between when we talk," Dianne said, sounding a little annoyed. "You record and then play it back later to see if you caught anything."

"I've heard of that," the blonde-haired girl chimed in. "From watching *Ghost Adventures*."

Dianne lit up with a smile. "Absolutely! One of my favorite shows!"

"Finally," Megan said, "someone to share in my sister's love of all things ghosts."

The blonde girl laughed and said, "Yeah, it creeps me out, but it's really interesting. I know they do EVP stuff, and they also use that spirit box thing where they cycle through the radio channels really fast to see if they hear any messages coming through. Have you tried that before?"

"No," Dianne said. "I'd like to, though. One day I wanna go on a full ghost investigation with cameras and all that. Lock myself in a haunted house for a night."

"Oh, I don't think I could do that," the blonde girl said. "I'm already freaked out being in here, and it's not even sundown yet."

As if to illustrate her point, her boyfriend snuck up behind her and grabbed her shoulders, making her jump a little. "Hey! That's not funny!" She slapped him on the arm as he returned a big grin.

Dianne swung her phone around until it was in the center of the living room, above the wooden coffee table that sat before the fireplace. She crouched down, feeling for a presence, looking to find the spot where Lily was playing before she went to the kitchen to get stabbed to death.

"Are you picking up anything?" Megan asked. "Do you hear the little girl's voice?"

"No, I told you, we go back and—"

From the bottom of the staircase, Michelle said, "If you're not already feeling creepy vibes from this place, just wait until it gets dark." The guide sounded like she was talking indirectly to Megan. "In about half an hour, when we're gonna be making contact, I'm sure all of you will be picking up on things, hearing things, all that. I can tell you, being in this house can make any skeptic a believer."

Dianne looked over at her sister, and although she couldn't hear it, she knew Megan was saying in her mind, "Sure, I'll be a believer. I'll believe it when I see it!"

Chapter 11

The Doctors' Quarters

The rain had stopped. For that, Dianne was thankful. However, a chill covered the air. It didn't help that Dianne was damp. All her clothes were heavy and cold. There was no way she wasn't going to be sick after all this. Maybe the flu, perhaps pneumonia. Between the chill and being around all the grit and filth of the hospital, Dianne was covered head to toe in germs. Ancient bacteria. Dust, maybe even asbestos. No matter the case, she had to keep going.

With the night sky cleared for the moment, Dianne could see the grounds under the light of the moon, which peaked between passing clouds. She looked across to the darkened buildings, the gate to her right, the security post to her left. It took a second as she assessed the environment again, but Dianne realized that the Administration Building was gone. The rest of the grounds seemed to be how she left them, but the building that used to stand in the center had disappeared.

Of course, Dianne thought after the sight of the empty lot set in. *It was only a matter of time.* With the holes appearing in Wing A, along with the staircase falling apart and the appearing and vanishing patients and nurses, Dianne couldn't be too surprised that another piece of Shaded Grove Mental Hospital was missing, although it was disheartening to know that the only landline in the whole place vanished as well. Then again, Dianne wondered if the phone would've worked anyway or if it was just an illusion made of dust that would crumble in her hand once the power came back on. That was if the power outage itself was real. Todd. The generator. The nurse. The keys. What would Dianne do if *none* of it was real?

The thought gave her an idea.

Dianne went to the metal gate, moving slowly along the concrete path with her flashlight still turned off. Her eyes had adjusted well-enough in the moonlight to guide herself and Dianne wasn't looking to stand out with a bright beam as she walked around the grounds. The more hidden she was from the spirits, the better, although she wondered how much longer it would be until she had no choice but to interact with a ghost.

At the gate, Dianne grabbed one of the rusty bars and gave it a good shake. She hoped the metal would crumble in her palm but found no such luck. There was also no sign of anyone on the other side. The parking lot was vacant.

Dianne went into the nearby toll booth, where she found no help from the small set of controls on the counter. The buttons didn't work, and she was still without the gate key to place in the tiny opening beneath the thin window. Her mind went back to Todd's post beyond what used to be the Administration Building, all the keys she spilled on the floor. She couldn't remember if she ever did find the one for the main gate. Maybe it was among the others.

Dianne returned to the concrete paths, retracing her

steps to the security post. The route took her to the new patch of tall grass that stood in place of the Administration Building. For a moment, Dianne turned her flashlight on to shine its beam on the wet grass. It was as if the building never existed at all or, if it did, nature already grew over any remnants of a brick-laid foundation. She had to move on before the rest of the place turned into nothing more than overgrown grass.

Following the curved concreate path, Dianne started to smell smoke lingering in the air. She kept her light on as she checked the surrounding area, looking to see if there was a fire anywhere, but Dianne didn't see any flames or even the haze of smoke around her. The grounds were the same except for the scent. It reminded her of her Uncle Tommy, her mother's brother, who was a heavy smoker. Whenever the Willis girls went to his apartment to visit, or he came over to their house for the holidays, they'd get a good whiff of the stale, smokey scent that clung to his clothes and breath. His teeth and fingernails always had a yellow tinge to them. Dianne would kill to have her uncle around right now to get her and Megan out of this mess, smelly or not.

Dianne turned the flashlight off until she was inside the security post across from Wing A. Once there, she lit up the concrete room to see, as far as she could tell, the place was unchanged. The desk was still there, cluttered like before. The key box remained, along with the multiple keys scattered on the floor below it. Dianne knelt, collecting them all as she searched for any label that read nurse's station or something similar.

The key with the most legible label read: QUARTERS. Dianne pocketed it along with the rest of the others that were littered all around her. Taking all of them and shoving them into her jeans wasn't the best method since she didn't have a key ring to keep them all together, but it was better to have every option she could. More was better than less.

Dianne also raided the desk, searching the entirety of it and its drawers for any additional keys, but found nothing of any use. *Of course.* There was hardly anything of use in the old hospital. Every turn, every path led to another messy issue, another dirty room. Getting out would be no easy feat.

Back outside, the smoke continued to swirl across the night and Dianne's nose. It didn't smell stronger, but the nostalgic, familiar scent wasn't going away anytime soon. It hung in the chilled air, almost as if to beckon Dianne toward the source, wherever that was.

That nurse, she thought. *Nurse Grantham...* Dianne remembered her tapping on something before she walked out of Wing A. *Cigarettes.* She didn't turn off her flashlight as she motioned it from her right to her left, going from Wing A, the metal gate, Wing B, and then the buildings labeled: DOCTORS' QUARTERS.

Where did that nurse go?

Dianne was conflicted in her mind. Part of her wanted to rush back to Room 222 and shove every last key she had into the lock until she got through. Another part drew her to the smoke, giving her the theory that Nurse Grantham was somewhere close, having a cigarette on her break. If Dianne found her, maybe she could get another key or, if she was extra nice to the spirit, she could get her to help directly, have her free Megan from the second floor without causing any trouble. If not the nurse, maybe someone else. Todd or another character that lurked on the grounds. *Anyone. Anything.* Dianne couldn't return to her sister empty-handed.

Dianne walked back toward the patch of grass that

replaced the Administration Building and stood in the center of Shaded Grove Mental Hospital, between Wing A and the Doctors' Quarters. In front of her was the gate. To the left of that, Wing B, and behind her, the security post. She felt like every building inside the barbed wire fenced facility was staring at her, looming over her with dreadful energy, like she was standing in the middle of a monster's mouth and the teeth were about to snap shut and crunch on her whole body until it swallowed her whole, leaving her inside the belly forever. She didn't like the feeling one bit. It was the heaviest weight she'd ever felt on a spiritual level. The darkness. The pain. The ominous energy poured from every corner of Shaded Grove.

The sound of rocks falling came from Dianne's left, toward the two Doctors' Quarters buildings. It sounded like one of the walls was falling apart. Dianne shot her light toward the quarters but didn't see anything or anyone around. Following the noise, she approached the two brick buildings with a thick strip of grass between them—it had a little white fence on the front end. From where Dianne stood with her flashlight, the smell of smoke grew stronger.

As she stood still for a moment, trying to calculate her next move, Dianne heard faint voices talking from beyond the brick walls. There was a deep, masculine voice followed by another—a woman. Dianne couldn't decipher the conversation, and it was getting harder to hear as her heart rate elevated again, making it sound like her heart was pounding between her ears.

Dianne moved toward the window by the door but kept low in case someone was watching her from inside. She was going to make herself known to the spirits; that was her intention, but only fools rushed in blindly, right? Dianne wanted to observe the spirits a bit first to get a feel for the energy surrounding them. *Reading the room,* she thought.

She clicked off her flashlight as she crouched with her head almost touching the bricks. Her head lifted slowly until her eyes were leveled with the bottom of the window. There wasn't much to see. It was too dark beyond the glass.

Dianne fumbled around in her pocket, clicking on and off her flashlight as she searched the fistful of keys for the one that read QUARTERS underneath the faded word that must've read DOCTORS at some point.

When she found the proper key after a few moments of shuffling them around, Dianne crept to the white door beside her and slid the key into the lock in the middle of the brass knob as the faint voices continued inside.

The door squeaked on its hinges. Dianne opened it slowly but held the knob tight as she felt it start to wobble like it was going to pop out any second and make a loud clang on the ground.

The smoke was as potent as ever as Dianne entered a dark hallway. There was no waiting room or receptionist desk when she stepped inside, only a line of closed doors with smoked glass staring back at her. She wasn't sure if it was the type of privacy glass that gave them the murky look or if every room was filled with actual smoke. It sure smelled like it.

Dianne kept her light off and her steps silent as she crouched again, moving toward the farthest door on the right. Although inside the building now, she couldn't tell which room the voices were coming from. To her, it sounded like they could be behind any of the doors. So, like a twisted game show, Dianne would have to reveal the prize or punishment behind every door until she found what she was looking for.

Moving along the carpeted floor, Dianne reached for the far-end door's knob. It was locked. She tried the key she used for the front door and, to her surprise, found that it worked. For the first time ever, she had a key that unlocked more than one lock. If only the key to Wing A did the same thing, then she could free Megan from the room with no problem.

There was no one inside the rectangular room that held a small single mattress and desk with a shattered ashtray on it. Everything was trashed, lonesome. Holes were in the ceiling, the walls. However, Dianne started to make out some of the words spoken by the man and woman hidden in the building. Something about a patient. Unbelievable behavior. Anger. A mention of a woman.

Dianne went back out into the hall, crouched as she moved to the second door, which was already unlocked. It led her to a similar room with the same layout of a bed and a single desk across from each other. Messy. Smoky. Filled with holes, just like in Wing A. The voices became clearer. Dianne could almost hear it fully now, something about a drug. New methods of testing. Still, she needed to find the ghosts and listen to what they were going on about. She needed to see them face to face.

In the third room, the second to last door in the hall, Dianne went in to find no furniture inside. It was empty except for the holes. Those things were everywhere now, forming just before Dianne could see them, like they appeared only in the corner of her eye.

One of the holes at the bottom of the left wall was where Dianne could hear the conversation crystal clear from the last room in the hallway. Before she went next door to confront the spirits on the other side, she approached the opening and listened to the back and forth between the mysterious couple. Dianne listened in as the man spoke first. Not only could she hear his words, but the flicking of a lighter as well. Drags on a cigarette. Blowing smoke.

"...I just don't know what to do," the man said with a sigh. "I feel like every time I take one step forward, I end up taking three back. I'm just running around in circles with her."

"I wish there was more I could do for you," the woman replied.

"I appreciate that, but the truth is there's a whole lot we don't understand. To have a woman like her, a full-grown adult lashing out with such violence, is . . . disheartening, to say the least. It's like this unstoppable force that comes over her. Completely contrasts her other behavior."

"Right, I've seen that," the woman said. "To be honest with you, I don't think any of the other patients have it as severe as she does." She exhaled. Dianne smelled more smoke pouring through the hole. "I often have to keep myself under control, so I don't retaliate unprofessionally. Sometimes it gets to the point where I almost have to use self-defense. At what point *do* you defend yourself? When the outbursts become a threat to your life?"

There was a pause in the conversation, leaving only the sounds of the man and woman puffing on their cigarettes for a moment.

"Imagine what her family must've gone through," the woman said, breaking the silence. "Her poor children. Makes you wonder if it's only a matter of time before one of them must be admitted. If not for having the same outbursts, the mental damage done by being around that kind of rage."

"It's rather sad, isn't it?"

"It is. Very sad."

Another pause. More puffs. More smoke. It stung Dianne's nose--the acrid smell was even harsher than any time she spent with her Uncle Tommy or when her mother used to light up after a stressful day when she was younger. Dianne was about to go back into the hallway and enter the neighboring room to confront the man and woman.

"Do you think... Do you think there may be no cure for patients like her?" the man asked. His tone was depressed, the question deflating him.

"No cure?" the woman replied, almost in a whisper.

"Correct, and I'm not even just talking about the one patient," the man said. "I'm talking about everyone currently admitted, everyone we've discharged. When I'm taking a moment for myself and reflect on my days here, I sometimes wonder if what we're doing is providing any real help."

"Of course, Doctor, we're—"

"I know we're pumping them with medications. Shocking them. Giving them insulin shots as they sleep. But I'm talking on a deeper level, not merely masking the symptoms or giving them a few moments where they are not of sound mind. I'm talking about their spirits. Their souls. Do you think we're doing anything to fix those parts of these patients?"

"I think so," the woman answered. "I agree that there's a lot we may not understand about the human mind, but I think we're doing the best we can with what we have. It's not like they're all helpless. If you really want my opinion, I believe there are different levels of illnesses. Different severities."

"Their souls, Alyssa, their souls," the doctor said with a

raised voice. Not angry, just loud. "You and I are on the same page when it comes to the textual definitions of the mind, the sicknesses that plague the chemical makeup. What I'm talking about is their being. The invisible force inside of them. Are we doing anything about that? Or I guess a better way to frame it is: is there any way *to* fix a fractured soul?"

Alyssa didn't say anything. As much as Dianne was frightened as she eavesdropped by the hole in the wall, the question was an interesting one.

"Maybe I'm just out of my mind. Maybe I'm not thinking right," the doctor said. "Sleep-deprived."

"I understand what you mean, but you do need to rest. It's exhausting enough having to care for these patients. Without sleep, you're bound to burn yourself out."

"Yeah, but it makes me question this whole operation. If what we're doing is the right thing, or if we're doing more harm than good, especially to those we keep in the basements. They're like prisoners down there... I don't even know what will ultimately happen to them. It's like with that woman. If she's acting this violently now, she may have to join the others and get more sedative treatments," the doctor said, his voice lowering back into a defeated tone. "Do you think decades from now, the future generations will look back at what we've done and be repulsed at our methods?"

"I don't know," Alyssa replied. "But we can't worry about that. Whatever will come will come. There's no way to predict the future and what advances will be made in medicine. We simply must work with what we have and hope that we acquire new knowledge along the way."

"Right..."

There was another sound of a lighter flicking.

"Why don't I put on some music to help you relax," Alyssa said as the sound of her footsteps went across the room. A creaky lid lifted. The vintage crackling of a vinyl record playing filled the air until a voice sang through a fading speaker in the other room.

Put your head on my shoulder...

Hold me in your arms, baby...

Squeeze me oh-so-tight...

Show me that you love me too...

Dianne exited the room and quick-stepped to the final door to the hall. It was locked. Dianne had to dig out the QUARTERS key from her pocket again and click her flashlight back on as the music continued beyond the smoked-glass door.

Put your lips next to mine, dear...

Won't you kiss me once, baby...

Just a kiss goodnight, maybe...

The key didn't work. Out of all the doors in the hallway, *this* was the one where the key wouldn't slide into the knob.

"Hello?" Dianne said into the door. "Could you please let me in?" She started knocking.

No response came from either the doctor or Alyssa from the other side, only the sound of an old 1950s tune, one that you'd hear in a diner back in the day.

People say that love's a game...

A game you just can't win...

If there's a way...

Dianne started banging on the glass. She yanked on the knob. "I need your help. Please let me in!"

No answer.

Put your head on my shoulder...

In her desperation, Dianne kicked against the door

before she backed up and ran shoulder-first into the wood. It hurt like hell, but Dianne didn't have time to register the pain as she backed up again and slammed into the door, this time breaking away some of the wood around the frame, making loud snapping and cracking sounds.

Tell me, tell me that you love me too...

The door broke open. Chunks of wood flew. Dianne almost fell flat on her face as her body pushed through, but she caught herself before she fell onto the stained carpeted floor.

Inside, the doctor sat at the desk beside the record player in the corner. Alyssa was on the edge of the mattress across from it. Both of them were staring at Dianne, unmoving, not speaking. They each held a lit cigarette between their fingers. Tiny tufts of smoke twirled from their lit ends.

Put your head on my shoulder...

Shoulder...

Shoulder...

The record skipped as Dianne approached the doctor with her flashlight shining into his cloudy eyes that sat behind thick metal glasses. He had a grayed beard, bold eyebrows, and wore a lab coat that must've once been white before turning into a yellowed tinge. By the breast pocket, it read: DR. HENRY GRAY. He stared back at Dianne without moving an inch.

"Can you hear me?" Dianne asked as her light reflected off the lenses of Dr. Gray's glasses.

Shoulder...

Shoulder...

Shoulder...

Dianne turned to look at Alyssa. Nurse Alyssa Grantham to be exact. She had dark-brown hair and cat-eyed glasses. She looked somewhat youthful in her old school nurse's outfit. The long bottom. The apron. Her white hat was sitting beside her on the bed. Much like the doctor, she only stared back at Dianne, frozen like a statue with a cigarette burning toward her long fingers.

"I just need your help. I'm not here to disturb you," Dianne said, which was a funny thing to say considering she literally broke down the door to get to them.

Shoulder...

Shoulder...

Shoulder...

Holes riddled the room. Dark spots. Stains from unknown substances. Even the record player beside the desk looked like it was moments away from falling apart from the rotting wood that encased the vinyl spinning beneath the rusted speaker.

Shoulder...

Shoulder...

Shoulder...

"I'm looking for the key to Room 222 in Wing A," Dianne said, facing Nurse Grantham on the filthy bed. "Could you help me? My sister is stuck in there."

The nurse stared. The cigarette burned closer to the filter.

"Please..." Dianne moved her flashlight up and down the nurse until she found pockets on either side of her apron. "Do you have it with you? I really need to get back to my sister."

No reply came from Nurse Grantham. Dianne shot a glance back at the doctor, who stared at her like his eyes were two surveillance cameras.

"What can I do to get my sister out?" Dianne asked with panic injected into her voice. She turned back to the nurse. "I'll do anything, whatever it takes to get us out of here. We didn't mean to come here. I'm sorry if we disturbed you."

The nurse gave nothing in return—not a movement nor sound came from her.

Shoulder...

Shoulder...

Shoulder...

Dianne sighed before she shined her light on Nurse Grantham's pockets again. She felt so uncomfortable doing it, but she had no choice. Dianne reached down and placed her left hand in the first pocket of the nurse's apron. However, before Dianne's fingers could reach the opening, Nurse Grantham's head fell from her neck and exploded into a cloud of dust in her lap.

Dianne screamed and jumped back from the nurse, bumping into the knees of Dr. Gray, which caused them to crumble into ashes. She tumbled backward, falling onto the doctor's body, crushing it instantly as if he were made of nothing more than a pillar of dust.

Shoulder...

Shoulder...

Shoulder...

The room filled with ashy clouds. Dianne coughed and wheezed, waving her arm out before her to clear the dust from her face. It was thick as it floated all around, getting into Dianne's mouth, eyes, and hair. She had to roll away from the desk to get any relief from the blinding dust.

Her light could still penetrate somewhat through the hanging particles, but she decided to back herself into the hallway to catch her breath.

When she stood up and went toward the front door of the building, Dianne tasted a stale sheen on her tongue. She spat onto the carpet before she opened the entrance door and leaned her head out into the chilly night to breathe in the fresh air. The coolness helped her get clean oxygen into her lungs, but she couldn't help but cough and spit up dark phlegm onto the ground as the skipping record continued behind her.

Shoulder...

Shoulder...

Shoulder...

Dianne zipped her jacket down a few inches so she could pull her shirt up and over her nose. She had to scrunch her neck so the shirt's collar would stay up. Dianne would've liked to have a pair of goggles or a mask to cover her face better, but she had to work with what she had.

Back inside the Doctors' Quarters, Dianne walked slowly to the broken door frame at the far end of the left side of the hall. She saw the dust particles still dancing through the opening, but she could get closer without having a coughing fit.

Shoulder...

Shoulder...

Shoulder...

Through the haziness, Dianne saw an empty chair in front of the desk. A cloud of dust. A pile of dark ashes. The lone lab coat. Nurse Grantham's headless body still sitting on the edge of the bed, the cigarette just about finished.

Dianne walked into the room and fanned as much dust as she could away from her squinting eyes. Nurse Grantham sat on the mattress, her body pale, mannequin-esque. With her head off and crumbled across her apron, there was no blood, no bodily fluids spurting from the hole in her neck. It was just a fleshy opening. Dianne was happy the scene wasn't as graphic as it should've been, but she was not interested in investigating what was inside the nurse's hollow body. Instead, she trained her focus toward the pockets by the apron again, this time being as careful as ever not to make any more limbs fall away.

Shoulder...

Shoulder...

Shoulder...

Some of the dust particles that clung to Dianne's collar penetrated through the fabric of her shirt. She cleared her throat and then blew air from her mouth, trying to push them away, but that ended up making the clouds go up into her eyes.

I have to be calm. I have to just get this over with and get out. Her heart thudded.

With her hand trembling like a leaf in the wind, Dianne dug her hand into one of the nurse's pockets. Then, without it being a surprise to Dianne, the entirety of Nurse Grantham's body collapsed into itself, along with the cigarette between her fingers. Its tiny ember disappeared into the cloud of ashes. All that remained was her clothes. The apron. The shirt and long skirt. Dianne kept her eyes shut tight and held her breath as she felt around the rubble of the nurse's remnants for any key she could find.

Shoulder...

Shoulder...

Shoulder...

The clumps of dust were cold and filthy between Dianne's fingers. She felt like she was stuffing her hand into the biggest pile of dryer lint in the world. It was unpleasant, but Dianne's fingers eventually found something hard amongst the dirty ashes covering the tattered mattress and old nurse's uniform.

It was hard to see in the haze of the dust cloud, but Dianne felt the brass key in her ashy palm just as she caught sight of it. The sight gave her a jolt of adrenaline and hope, but she wasn't ready to leave the Doctors' Quarters just yet. Dianne had to keep feeling around to make sure she had everything from the nurse. If she left with a single key and it didn't open either the nurse's station or Room 222 itself, the mission was a failure.

Shoulder...

Shoulder...

Shoulder...

Dianne coughed and choked on the blankets of dust that caked her face. She imagined her lungs were struggling against the ashy substance as she breathed in under her shirt. There were only so many seconds she could hold her breath. Dianne also kept her eyes shut. The dust stung them even if she peeked for a few moments.

Under the nurse's apron, Dianne felt another hard object among the ashes. She picked it up and shook off what she could. Through her burning, squinting eyes, Dianne made out another key similar in shape to the first one she plucked from the rubble, although she couldn't tell what the label said. She placed it in her pocket along with the other. Whenever she had a moment, Dianne would have to organize the various keys she had stuffed into her jeans.

Shoulder...

Shoulder...

Shoulder...

After a few more moments of blindly sifting through the ashes, Dianne's cough grew relentless. With the constant rain of dust, she was getting to the point where she was about to vomit as nausea swirled inside of her. It was time to leave the room and take in more breaths of fresh air outside before she blew chunks all over the murky room.

Almost stumbling to the floor, Dianne reached out in

front of her to grab the wall. She wasn't going to open her eyes until she escaped the Doctors' Quarters. Dianne coughed. Her throat burned. Everything spun behind her watering eyes.

Shoulder...

Shoulder...

Shoulder...

Dianne made it back to the hallway. The nausea wouldn't give. She placed a hand over her shirt-covered mouth and pressed forward until she felt the front door of the building. Dianne pushed it open and escaped to the hospital grounds as the Doctors' Quarters building began to tremble on its foundation. Dianne opened her eyes, blinked rapidly, and turned back to see the roof falling apart. She shined her light across the bricks and saw the holes growing larger. The same went for the neighboring quarters building, shaking and crumbling from the top down.

Dianne pulled the collar of her shirt down as she gasped in big gulps of chilly air. She sprinted back toward Wing A as the two Doctors' Quarters buildings lost their roofs, sending a plume of dust into the night sky. Dianne kept moving, breathing, coughing, as the walls fell next, crumbling into each other like dominos made of ashes. They vanished into one another, adding another layer of dirty particles into the rising cloud. There was one final echo of *shoulder..., shoulder..., shoulder...,* until the repeating voice on the vinyl record stopped for good.

Dust stained Dianne's tongue, sticking to the back of her throat. She needed water, anything to wash it away and get it out. It was so bitter, so thick inside of her mouth that not even her spit gave her the relief she needed as she tried to cough onto the concrete path below her. Nausea crashed through her in waves.

She couldn't fight it anymore. Dianne got down on her knees and threw up into one of the patches of tall grass by the pathway. It burned and tasted like the acrid digestion of burger and fries from the meal she had earlier in the day, but it rid the back of her throat and tongue from the sheen of ashes they had.

Dianne gagged and heaved as more brownish liquid flew from her mouth and sprayed the dark grass. Tears streamed down her cheeks. She was reliving the first night she ever got blackout drunk with her friends. Having too many shots of Fireball whiskey led her to this position before, kneeling, vomiting, and crying, although she had someone hold her hair in the past. Now, she was all by herself, hurling in an abandoned mental hospital some-where in the rural lands of Pennsylvania with her sweaty, wet hair sticking to her face.

Despite the pain from her throat and the awful taste that covered her taste buds, Dianne was thankful for the night's cool breeze. A gentle chill swiped at her face, making the disgusting experience just a little easier to get through. Whenever she got upset or fell ill like this, her whole body would get overheated.

The cloud of dust from the fallen Doctors' Quarters crept up behind Dianne. She didn't notice it at first, but when she whipped her hair away and swiped at her lips, she saw the haze approaching. She spat out another bitter piece of phlegm and got up from the concrete, not wasting time with her quick steps toward Wing A. Dianne wanted to avoid the flying ashes, not only because of the dangers they were to her health, but because there was a presence inside. She felt like every hanging cloud of dust was made up of the spirits that roamed the hospital grounds. Gerald Swaggart. Nurse Grantham. Dr. Gray. They might be broken away from the physical realm, but the dark dust that lingered kept their energy among the land of the living. To Dianne, the approaching haze was their last resort. If she stopped and let the filthy fog consume her, there was no telling where the phantoms would take her.

Chapter 12

The Pictures

Megan had no idea how prisoners could do it, how they could survive sealed inside of a room for such a long time. She wasn't even in Room 222 for more than two hours, and she was already going berserk. The fact that men and women were behind bars for years, sometimes for the rest of their lives, seemed beyond torture to her—complete insanity. Then again, prisoners didn't have to deal with the supernatural, did they?

"Let me out of here!" she screamed from the center of the room. "I want out!"

The metal box flashlight shot around the peeling walls. Megan had been searching every inch of the room for a hole to appear, any indication that there was a way out. However, her constant checking brought her no luck. Everything in Room 222 remained the same since she arrived.

"Goddammit! Let me out!"

The laughing woman didn't come back, which was nice at least. Megan could keep her pulse somewhat calmed since the mysterious pounding and chuckling went away.

No other characters came by. No scary entities appeared from thin air. For that, she was thankful.

"Dianne! Where are you?"

Part of Megan's outburst was to keep the noises away if they did happen to return. There was a strange comfort in only hearing her own voice in the broken room instead of laughter or strange whispers in the dark. She'd rather shred her throat with her yelling and shatter her eardrums from her own tantrum than get herself worked up from another visitor that wasn't her sister.

"Hello?"

Megan had to stop for a moment to catch her breath. She'd been screaming nonstop since the female laughter ceased, and the sound of her voice turned scratchy, like she had just finished chain-smoking a pack of cigarettes.

After a few harsh, heavy breaths, Megan reached down into the pile of the rubble by the corner and grabbed a sliced-open chair cushion, throwing it against the wooden door. She took a piece of a bed frame and chucked that as well.

"Piece of ...," she said under her breath. "Stupid door..."

Megan threw anything she could get her hands on. Pieces of cardboard. A wheel with a bit of plastic sticking out of the top. She was so fired up, so out of her mind, that she almost launched the flashlight, too.

"I'm gonna get out of here if it's the last thing I do!"

But her rage didn't last long. Megan found herself exhausted after a couple of minutes passed of her throwing various items toward the unbreakable door. The last thing she chucked, a light-pink lamp with no bulb or shade, went soaring into the bathroom as her strength diminished. The glass of the lamp met the porcelain of the toilet, shattering in an instant.

Megan broke down, this time with despair rather than rage. She went to her knees, placing the flashlight beside her on the floor. Her whole body shook as she wept. The pain in her elbow made itself known again, sending jolts up to her shoulder. She leaned forward with her hands covering her filthy, tired face. Megan didn't care how dirty her fingers and palms were.

She thought about her sister, how she was probably in a similar situation. Lost. Defeated. Trapped. Megan cried for her, wishing she could take it all back, wishing she was a better sister to Dianne. The arguments. The snarky attitude. The ridicule. The constant sarcasm and jokes.

Perhaps the pain was in her all along. Maybe Megan's lifelong aggressive behavior was all just a mask to hide her real feelings deep down inside. Sadness. That every time she pushed someone away with her attitude was a defense mechanism to not let anyone in, to keep them away from what was behind the mask itself. The true identity of Megan Willis, a frightened, lonely girl. A girl who'd been hurt. Neglected. Abandoned. She had to become a no-nonsense kind of person to dig herself out of the grave that circumstances made for her. But that didn't get her anywhere. When push came to shove, she broke down and fell back into the core of what she was, which wasn't much different than her sister.

Dianne was shy, open-minded, and always searching her soul for the next revelation. Megan wanted to do the same but couldn't bring herself to admit it. Instead, she blocked the spiritual desires out and went toward the cynical, realistic approach even though the truth was she just wanted to have something or someone to believe in.

She loved her boyfriend, Gage, or she thought she did. Megan wasn't entirely sure. He was like her in the sense that he didn't allow himself to be vulnerable. Gage was tough and had a similar attitude toward life as Megan did, or at least how she appeared to have. Did Gage love her back, or did he have the same doubts when he searched deep into his heart as well?

Maybe Megan was more in love with the *idea* of being in love. The desire to love someone and the human need to be loved in return. She loved her mother and sister for sure. That's why even though she always gave them a hard time, Megan stuck around. Sure, it was no secret that Megan hated stupid, gimmicky nonsense like a ghost tour in the middle of nowhere, but she still drove her sister over an hour away to take part in it. She knew Dianne hated having to hear all her older sister's "real, raw thoughts," but Dianne didn't walk away from the siblinghood. She toughed it out and dealt with it because that's what family does. That's what real love is. Tolerance. Determination. Dedication. All of that even in the face irritancy. Disagreement. Times of anger and disappointment. That kind of love is steadfast, an unbroken bond forged from bedrock.

But what about the other kind of love? The passionate love. Being *in* love. Did Megan have that with Gage? Was it too soon to say? How long do you have to wait until you feel you're building that bedrock with someone? Is it even possible when you were born from broken glass yourself?

It was all too much to think about. Megan didn't even want to think about it, but her mental breakdown flooded her mind from all angles. Being trapped in Room 222 was enough for her psyche to overload her with emotions she wasn't ready to face yet.

As Megan stewed in her sorrow on the rotten floor, she was unaware of the sounds of trickling water coming from the bathroom. A puddle formed around the base of the stained toilet and remnants of the shattered lamp. Dark water flowed out from the bottom of the smashed porcelain, growing wider in size by the second.

The puddle moved, shifting into a stream that crept across the dusty tiles on the bathroom floor until it crossed over the doorway's line. It soaked up the grit, collecting the filth until it floated on top of the water's surface as it slithered toward Megan like a serpent.

Megan only saw the blackness from her closed eyelids. She only felt the pressure of her palms against her face. It wasn't until after a minute or so that something wet came across her knees, soaking through her already damp jeans.

She lifted her head up from her hands, her black hair dangling in a messy mop. The flashlight was still turned on beside her. Megan picked it up as she stood from her kneeling position, first inspecting her pants before the light's beam moved to the floor to see the murky water crossing the room. She followed the trail to see it coming from inside the bathroom.

"What the...?" Megan said to herself. The flashlight shined on the cracked toilet. She saw water coming up from the floor as well as the bottom base of the red and brown-stained porcelain.

Megan backed up as she noticed the water heading toward her boots. She shined her light toward the door but found no one looking through the window.

"Hello?"

No one answered her. Only the sound of the trickling dirty water remained.

The smell of feces rose from the floor as Megan backed away from the stream. In the light, she saw the water growing thicker, blacker. Whether it was ancient fecal matter or tar, Megan didn't know. She just wanted to get out of the room before the putrid liquid came any closer.

The door to Room 222 remained locked tight, unmoving against Megan's frantic pushes and pounds. She relentlessly knocked on the wood despite the pinging pain shooting through her elbow.

"Let me out!" she cried. "Please!" Megan hoped the laughing woman would return and show her mercy by magically swinging the door open, but Megan found no cackling savior on the other side.

She turned from the door and trained her light on the black water, which pooled in the center of the room. The darkness of the liquid contrasted with the brown grit of the tiles. The water was somehow dirtier than the room itself, smellier than any trashed corner.

Megan plugged her nose as the stench wreaked havoc on her senses, too potent to breathe in. She then covered her entire nose and mouth with the damp sleeve of her leather jacket. It provided a little better protection against the nasty scent as nausea built up inside her stomach. Things were getting beyond bad, and Megan had no options. That was until she realized the only way to possibly put an end to the building water was to stop it at its source: the vile bathroom.

She didn't want to do it at first. Hesitation seized her steps, but Megan knew that if she didn't get moving, there would be nothing left but to die in the pool of black tar water. As disgusting as it smelled in Room 222, Megan had to tough it out if she ever wanted to see her sister again, if she ever wanted to see her mother or Gage again.

Her boots splashed in the stream. It was like Megan was walking up a creek in the woods, except the creek was made up of foul, dark substances. She thought she would puke at any moment as the fumes wafted against her covered face.

Megan tried to keep her flashlight from shining on anything too repulsive, but just about every inch of the bathroom was flooded with sewage. The bottom of the toilet had an enormous gash on the side, the main source of the flowing water. Megan turned and returned to the room, searching for anything to clog it.

With one hand clutching the flashlight and the other wrapped around her face, Megan held her breath and used her left hand to grab a piece of half-soaked wood from the floor. She moved with lightning speed, so she didn't get a deep whiff of the dead smell.

Megan chucked the wood onto the bathroom floor. It started to float, but with a fast foot, Megan stomped it down against the hole in the toilet. Filthy water splashed onto her boots and the bottom of her jeans. She immediately placed her left arm over her mouth again and took a deep breath while she held her mouth against the moist leather. Some of the putrid stench made it to her nostrils, but not enough to let her vomit fly.

The water spurted from the sides of the blocking wood. Megan angled it to prevent it from splashing up at her, but the flow seemed to be growing in speed and power, like Megan's attempt to clog the hole made the water angrier.

A quick geyser of black fluids pushed the piece of wood away from the hole and out of Megan's grip under her boot. Megan let out an *eek* and jumped back, almost falling on her butt.

Objects shot out of the toilet. White squares. Pieces of materials. Globby things. Papers. Everything flooded into the room until the geyser settled, and water stopped streaming out of the hole. Silence fell. All Megan heard was her heartbeat blasting in her ears as she stared at the rippling black water that strangely came to a stop.

With her jacket's sleeve still covering her face, and her flashlight hovering above the dark water, Megan left the bathroom with careful steps. She scanned over the various papers floating on the blackness. The chunks of metal. The snapped plastic bits. The papers. Megan was about to turn her attention away from them all when she noticed one of the items floating in the murky liquid was a photograph. In fact, there were multiple pictures that must've come from the hole in the bathroom.

Megan used her boot to slide the photographs out of the water and onto the dry tiles by the wall. The white frames around the pictures were stained, and the pictures themselves were faded, but Megan could make out the first photo of a baby sitting in a stroller on a sidewalk, smiling at the camera. Megan didn't recognize the baby, not that she should've anyway, but the fact that it came from the pipes below the toilet of a second-floor mental ward creeped her out.

The second photo was of another baby, splashing away in a kitchen sink. Megan was cautious to continue examining the pictures as she was worried something graphic was about to appear. Still, she couldn't help but be drawn to the third picture, which had both babies in the frame, although they weren't quite babies anymore, and they weren't strangers.

A chill ran up Megan's spine as she shined her light on the faded photo that depicted the very young versions of herself and her sister, Dianne. Megan looked about three, wearing pink overalls and standing on a red scooter, while a one-year-old Dianne sat in the nearby grass, holding up dandelions in each hand. Both sisters smiled ear to ear.

Megan's lip quivered. She couldn't talk to herself or even utter a sound as the dirtied childhood photo stared back at her. The feeling only got worse as more photos came from the water, showing Megan memories of herself and her sister.

First days of school. Sledding in the snow. Christmas mornings. Summers at the community pool. Every picture Megan pulled from the muck was a fun moment from the sisters' childhood, the last being the Willis sisters together at someone's birthday party. Megan and Dianne sat behind a picnic table with sparkly hats, blowing into papery whistles that unfolded and buzzed. It was a snapshot of a happier time. They all were, but this was the worst possible time to come across these moments down memory lane.

Chapter 13

The Ashford House Part III

The twin boys, John and Jack, were killed upstairs in their bedroom. Nancy had finished stabbing her daughter in the kitchen, and the voices in her head led her to take the same knife to the necks of her sons, who were upstairs doing their schoolwork at the time.

When Nancy entered their room with silent steps and slit John's throat from behind, Jack attempted to run. However, Nancy was sure to lock the door behind her so neither of the poor boys could escape. The twisted woman had Jack all to herself as she committed the horrific act yet again. And when she finished, she stayed in the locked bedroom with her dead twins until she heard her husband coming home downstairs.

Of course, the story got scarier to Dianne by the moment. She was sure to take pictures around every corner while running her so-called EVP recording on another app, hoping to catch a word or two from the lingering spirits of the Ashford twins or their demonic mother.

"People have felt powerful presences up here," Michelle said as she stood inside the bedroom where the boys were slaughtered. "We've had a psychic come in and explain that the souls of twins are very strong. When you have two, three, or more children that are born together, their souls are interlocked into a chain. When those souls pass from this world, it leaves a dent twice as big as if a single person were to pass. That's still the case even if only one of the twins passes away. That energy is still attached to the living sibling. Had either Jack or John lived through the attack, there would be no question that they would have their brother's spirit following them around day and night."

Dianne was sure that statement got Megan's BS alarm going off. Dianne had read about twin spirits not too long ago, but to a smart aleck like Megan, the concept may come across as a bit silly. Then again, the whole idea of ghosts was silly to her. To Megan, death was death. There was no after-life, no heaven or hell, no purgatory, and there certainly wasn't a mysterious limbo of dimensions where spirits were trapped until they could fully pass on.

"You ever seen one of the boys yourself?" the biker man asked in his raspy voice.

"Oh, I've seen every member of the Ashford family multiple times," Michelle replied, looking proud. "As for the twins, I've seen things thrown across this room, I've seen their faces in the window here, staring down at me as I was locking up outside. I've heard their footsteps running back and forth. Jack and John are very active spirits."

"Wow," the biker's wife said. "Not sure how I'd react to any of that kinda stuff. I don't think I've ever seen a full-blown ghost before, let alone attacked by one."

Her husband turned to her and said, "Didn't you say you saw your dead grandfather when you were a little girl?"

The biker woman shrugged. "Yeah, but I could've been dreamin'."

"Are you a psychic?" the blond-haired girl, who clutched her boyfriend's hand even tighter now, asked Michelle.

Michelle laughed a little and said, "I like to tell people that I'm a psychic-lite. I know the basics of the rituals, which we will all participate in in a moment, but I'm not...," she waved her arms up and down her body, "...fully invested into the psychic world. In other words, I haven't tapped into the full set of psychic-medium abilities, at least not on a natural level I was born into. Does that make sense? I look at it more like a part-time job. People like The Long Island Medium and John Edward are fully immersed in their psychic work. I'm still at the beginner level."

Everyone in the group nodded, including Megan. Dianne knew she was just playing along.

"The stuff we'll do downstairs can be done by any of you," Michelle said. "I just watched some YouTube videos the other day to learn a few new methods, but we will stick to the regular séance stuff tonight. The basics."

The group mingled around the twins' room for another minute or two before Michelle led everyone back into the hall and down the squeaky staircase to the darkened living area, where she lit a candle and had the biker man help her pull a circular table to the center of the room, before the fireplace.

An obvious mixture of anxiousness and excitement emanated from the tour-goers. The man with the glasses placed his camera on one of the end tables and aimed it at the center table. Dianne saved her first EVP and started a new recording just for the séance.

She tried to not think about her sister and her disinterest in the whole thing. Dianne knew Megan just wanted to get this over with. She was ready for the setup of sound effects and voices, which she believed would come from hidden speakers just out of the group's sight, maybe in the slats of the wall, or tucked away behind the corner chairs. Megan probably also wanted to see if any strings were attached to the table, perhaps a secret switch or lever underneath it for Michelle to engage when things were supposed to get scary and wild. Megan always told Dianne that these tours had to have a big finish, so the participants would tell all their friends and family to come by to keep the ghost gimmick funded. How else would Michelle make a living if there weren't any "paranormal experiences" to be had in the Ashford House? She had to give the visitors a little something better than dust orbs in their cell phone photos.

Michelle swiped across the tabletop, brushing off the thin layer of dust that covered it. She placed the lit candle in a brass holder and set it in the center before waving at everyone to gather around the soft, flickering flame.

"If anyone's uncomfortable, you don't have to do this," she said. "If you're a germaphobe or too freaked out about contacting the dead, you can just stand aside and watch since we're all going to lean forward and place our hands close together around the candle until we hold each other's hands once we make a connection."

"Like in the movies," the biker guy said.

"Yes, absolutely," Michelle replied. "Pretty common method here, nothing too spectacular. But it's effective, definitely effective."

Megan poked Dianne's side, but Dianne elbowed her sister away. It was a common tactic, even in her late teens, for Megan to jab at Dianne during inappropriate times to either embarrass her or get her in trouble. In the handful of times that the Willis sisters attended church, Megan would always try to sneak in a tickle on her sister during the quiet moments of the service. The pastor would say, "Now, let us bow our heads and pray," and Megan would start poking Dianne's side, causing her to fight the giggles as the nearby churchgoers grew irritated. Their mother was forced to separate them. Fortunately for Dianne, the childish game didn't work for Megan that time.

Everyone gathered around the table, wasting no time putting their palms down on the wooden top, just before the orange glow that was the only remaining light source in the dark living room. Even the frightened blonde-haired girl was quick to place her hands down.

"Now, I'll ask you all to close your eyes," Michelle said softly. "Try to keep your mind focused on the present. Let your thoughts pass you by as best as you can."

Dianne felt Megan stepping on her sneaker; her sister's hard boot digging down onto her toes. Dianne wiggled her foot, giving Megan a little kick under the table. There was nothing more exciting to Dianne than a séance, and having her older sister trying to interrupt the process was making her furious. Michelle had just instructed everyone to calm their minds. How could Dianne be calm when Megan was being so annoying? It was at times like these, when Megan acted anything but her age, that Dianne's typical positive vibe turned sour. No one knew how to get under the skin like a sibling, and Megan was doing just that, getting under Dianne's skin like a flesh-crawling virus, trying to burrow deeper until Dianne had no choice but to have an outburst.

But Dianne remained cool, calm, and collected as she forced herself to push her annoying sister out of her mind.

Michelle gave everyone a minute to settle themselves around the candle until she closed her eyes and went on with the seance. "We are calling out to you, Ashford family. We come to you from a time and place of peace. We are not looking to bring you any harm or any pain. We only wish to contact your spirits to get a better understanding of what you've been through."

Nothing happened.

"We call on the spirit of Nancy Ashford," Michelle said. "If you're here with us, please give us a sign."

Megan peaked under her eyelid, giving a quick glance around.

"Nancy," Michelle went on, "if you're with us, in this room, in this house, please make yourself known. We're not here to punish you."

The biker guy coughed. Megan slid her pinky finger past Dianne's left hand.

"We call on Ethan Ashford to make himself known. If your spirit is with us, Ethan, please give us a sign. We just want to talk to you."

After another bout of silence, Michelle continued to ask the spirits to appear. Lily. Jack and John. None of them made an appearance. No sounds. No nothing. After more time passed without any signs from the afterlife, Dianne grew disappointed, knowing if no paranormal experiences occurred, Megan would be giving her an earful, ranting about how the whole ghost tour was a waste of time and that Dianne's beliefs were a joke.

However, Dianne's feelings soon shifted as the dimly lit seance took an unexpected turn after Michelle started asking other questions.

"Are there any other spirits in this room with us?" Michelle asked. "Is there anyone that would like to speak to us? We are not here to cause you any harm."

The blonde-haired girl suddenly spoke. "Oh, my God. Does anyone else feel cold right now?"

Everyone except for Michelle opened their eyes and

glanced around the table. Confused fear painted each of their faces.

"You know what," the guy with the glasses said as he looked down at his sweater, "I'm starting to feel a little chilly myself."

Megan looked over at Dianne. Dianne didn't return a glance, not wanting to catch a glimpse of her sister's inevitable "this is stupid" face with rolled eyes and a dropped mouth.

"It's okay if your body starts to feel cold. Don't be alarmed," Michelle said, keeping her eyes shut. "They're not going to hurt you. It's just their way of saying they want to join us, that they want to be around us."

Nervous laughter came from the group. No one seemed to want to close their eyes again.

"Who is in this room with us?" Michelle asked as her head tilted back. She was in a semi-trance. "Can you tell us your name?"

The red-haired guy's eyes were trained on the candle's flame, hoping to see a sudden movement from it. Dianne felt her senses heightening.

"I'm starting to feel somethin', too," the biker's wife said. "I think I'm gettin' the heebie jeebies!"

"I'm sensing a presence," Michelle said before she flipped her palms up on the table. There was a slight sheen of sweat on her skin. "Let's grab onto each other for a moment and chain our energies together."

Everyone hesitated for a moment. Their initial eagerness faded away, and now the group of tour-goers was unsure if they should proceed after the sudden change in the living room's temperature. Whether they shared Megan's belief that this was a setup or not, they were a bit unsettled. Nonetheless, they all flipped their hands over and held the chilled, sweaty hands of the people on either side of them until the whole group formed a standing, linked circle around the table and candle. Everyone waited with bated breath as the seance continued.

Michelle was the only one to close her eyes again. "To the spirit or spirits in this room with us, we ask you to please come forward and tell us your names."

Nothing.

"You can trust us," Michelle said. "Use me as your vessel. Speak to me, give me a sign so I can call you by your name."

The only sound was a quick, faint creak on the hardwood floor. It made the blonde-haired girl and the guy with glasses flinch slightly. They both smiled and tried to settle themselves. The blonde girl's boyfriend whispered, "It's all right," in her ear.

"If you cannot tell us your name," Michelle said, her voice a little lower than before, "then can you give us a sign, anything to confirm your presence here with us."

The living room fell more silent than ever as everyone held their breath, waiting for something to happen.

And something did.

A cold wave of air blew into the room from the foyer, gliding across the bodies of the tour-goers, making the candle's flame wave and dance. An audible groan came from the group. The blonde girl's eyes widened in shock. Megan squeezed Dianne's hand. Dianne wasn't sure if it was genuine or not.

"Shh, shh," Michelle said. "Do not be afraid. We're safe, totally safe."

"You leave a window open or somethin'?" the biker guy asked, trying to force a nervous laugh behind his words.

Michelle shook her head. Her eyes remained closed as

she kept herself in her trance. "We feel you in this room, spirit. Thank you for making yourself known. But we would like to know your name. Where you come from. Who you are."

Half the group looked at the candle. The other half peered all around, trying to see the next ghostly sign before it had time to give them a jump.

"Yes. I can see it. I'm getting a symbol," Michelle said. "E... the letter E. In my mind's eye. E."

"The ghost's name is E?" the biker woman asked.

Michelle didn't say anything at first as her mouth opened slightly. She looked like she was nodding off until she said, "I can only see letters and numbers when I do this. Most of the time, the spirits only have so much energy they can send. They only have enough strength to push through with a symbol."

Another chilled breeze blew through the living room. The candle's flame waved but didn't extinguish. Dianne's hands started to tremble a bit. Her heart rate rose.

"W...," Michelle uttered. "I'm getting an E and a W."

"Ew," the blonde-haired girl said under her breath.

"They're trying to push through," Michelle said. "There's a spirit. I can sense.... I can sense someone older. E. W. I can hear...a woman's voice. She's trying to come closer. She says she's looking for someone," Michelle said. "Her energy is growing stronger. She's really trying to get to where we are."

"Oh, my God," the blonde-haired girl said.

"Who she lookin' for?" the biker man asked.

"E. W. I keep getting those letters," Michelle said. "She seems very serious. Angry even." Her eyes went back and forth beneath her lids. "Who are you looking for? Tell me.

Are they in this room with us? Are you being drawn to someone here?"

"I don't like this," the blonde-haired girl said. "I'm feeling really creeped out right now."

"Just relax," Michelle said. "Nothing to worry about. If you get too scared, just break from our chain. We can stop this communication at any time."

"Well, let's just see what happens now," the biker man said, sounding as if the blonde-haired girl's fear was an inconvenience. "I never spoke to a ghost before."

The blonde-haired girl's boyfriend looked like he wanted to break the chain himself and hug her to calm her down, but it was clear he was also intrigued by Michelle's performance.

"Is it...?" Michelle paused and leaned her head back some more. If she moved another inch like that, her whole body would fall. "Oh, it is..." Michelle's mouth dropped. "Someone in this room, you're here for someone in this room... Maybe more than one?"

Audible gasps came from the group.

"Who is it?" Michelle asked. "Can you tell me who you're here to make contact with?"

Silence.

"E. W." Michelle kept her head back, eyes closed. "Do those letters mean anything to anyone?"

Everyone looked around, shrugging.

"I'm getting a strong feeling of an elderly woman. Perhaps someone's grandmother or great-grandmother," Michelle said. "A distant relative. Maybe an ancestor from a time long ago. E. W."

"My grandma's been dead a while, but E and W don't mean nothin'," the biker's wife said. Her eyes darted around. "Least, I don't think so."

The guy with glasses' eyes were trained upwards as he stood deep in thought, trying to reach far back into his own family history.

"Give us a sign," Michelle said, "anything to show us who you're here for. Show us your presence using all the energy you can muster. We only wish to speak back to you."

Cold wind blasted the group from the center of the table. The candle's flame gave a final wave before vanishing into darkness, leaving only the smelly trail of smoke behind. The blonde-haired girl shrieked as the living room turned pitch-black.

"Holy shit!" the biker man shouted.

"What... what—" The guy with glasses couldn't finish his sentence as the wood floor began to tremble. Loud, heavy steps banged against the floor. It sounded like an elephant marching all around the group, just behind everyone in the circle, passing by each of them with a shadowed swiftness. It was such a sudden, powerful force that it felt like the entire Ashford House shook on its foundation.

The blonde-haired girl screamed again. The biker's wife cursed. Dianne squeezed Megan's hand hard. Megan jumped from sudden loud noises, swearing under her breath.

"It's all right. It's okay," Michelle said from the darkness. She flicked her lighter, illuminating her face in a faint light before placing the small flame on top of the smoking wick, bringing the candle back to life. For good measure, she grabbed more candlesticks from the corner of the living room and lit them, placing them throughout so the group could see better.

Everyone still held hands around the circular table except for the blonde-haired girl and her boyfriend, who were locked in an embrace by the window. The girl's face was buried in his sweatshirt, her eyes shut tight. She wasn't crying, but she looked like she was seconds away from having a mental breakdown.

"I'm sorry," Michelle said. "Sometimes things get like that, a little loud and frightening. But it's okay. The spirit is gone now. We've lost connection. That won't happen again. You're safe."

The blonde-haired girl pulled her face out of her boyfriend's chest. Even in the lights of the orange candles, the group could see she was as white as a ghost. "It's okay, I'm all right. That was just...really unexpected." She stuck her hands out in front of her. They trembled. "I think that's enough ghost stuff for me tonight."

"Yeah," her boyfriend said, rubbing her back. "I think we're gonna head out if that's all right."

"Absolutely." Michelle approached the couple. She spoke softly. "Thank you both so much for coming. I'm so sorry that I shook you up."

The couple both feigned smiles and started toward the door. The rest of the group wished the two of them well as they remained standing around the table with a mixture of both relief and disappointment. On the one hand, they were glad the young woman was getting out of the haunted house and away from the terrors of the séance. On the other, they were all still curious about how far the so-called E. W. spirit would go.

"It's getting pretty dark out there," Michelle said, following the couple. "Would you like me to walk you two to your car? I have a flashlight."

Without missing a beat, the blonde-haired girl and her boyfriend said, "No, thanks." It was clear that the two of them were itching to get as far away from Michelle and the Ashford House as possible.

"Be careful out there and thank you again for coming!" Michelle said as the couple exited through the front door with fast feet. The old porch whined beneath their frantic steps before the sounds of speedy sneakers on the gravel path followed.

"At least it stopped raining for the moment," she said under her breath as the two shadows of the couple vanished.

There was an awkward atmosphere that hung over the living room as Michelle returned to the group. The biker folks still held hands, waiting for Michelle to continue the séance. Both of their mouths quivered as if they both had something to say but couldn't get it out. The guy with glasses went over to the end table, where his camera was aimed at the circular table. He didn't touch it but instead hovered his head over the viewfinder and adjusted his black frames.

Meanwhile, Dianne and Megan stood on the opposite side of the biker couple, staring at each other with different expressions. Dianne had a serious, flat face, while Megan smiled ear to ear. Dianne didn't have to do too much thinking to know that her sister was having too much fun having just witnessed two people freak out and leave the ghost tour. The truth was, Dianne was about to ask Megan if she was ready to go, too, but was interrupted by Michelle.

"So, sometimes that happens," Michelle said, returning to the table. She wiped her hands on her pants. "It's not unusual for people to get overwhelmed and scared, especially if it's their first time trying to make contact."

"We weren't that scared," the biker man said before he shot a smile over to his wife. "Although when that candle blew out... Oh man!"

His wife nodded. "That was spooky as hell, Michelle! What did you think was gonna happen next?"

Michelle shrugged. "It's unpredictable. Every time is something new. I can tell you, during one of the tours during the summer, we had those heavy footsteps, but they were all above us."

"Was it the twins?" Dianne asked.

"I think so," Michelle said. "They were probably playing around up there as we did the séance down here. But you know, I think the scariest thing that's ever happened during one of these, at least for me, was when the candlestick itself started to float."

The biker woman's face dropped as Michelle reenacted the levitating candle.

"Wow," Megan said disingenuously.

After adjusting his camera and walking back over to the table in the center of the room, the guy with glasses said, "Getting back to the séance itself, you mentioned how they could only send you symbols. The E and the W." He turned and looked at the others. "I know none of us could think if the letters meant anything, but have you ever experienced someone making a connection with just the letters? Has anyone ever said they *did* mean something?"

"Absolutely," Michelle said as she put the candlestick back down on the wood. "I believe it was a woman in her mid-fifties. She was on this tour with her niece and nephew, and when I made contact with a spirit, I was given the letter X."

The biker couple flashed fascinated glances at each other.

"Pretty uncommon letter to get, I can tell you that," Michelle chuckled. "But believe it or not, this woman became hysterical and started screaming, 'Dad! Dad, is that you?'"

"Woah," the guy with glasses said.

"Turns out her recently deceased father was named Xavier," Michelle said, holding her hands up like she couldn't deny the fact. "Out of all the names, we make contact with a spirit with that specific letter."

"Did her father's ghost appear?" Dianne asked. "Was she able to communicate with him?"

"Only for a little," Michelle answered. "Spirits only have so much energy, and it gets weaker by the second. That's why I can only get those letters at first. Once the spirit starts a conversation, it's only a matter of time until they fade. However, I was able to tell her that her father was looking after her and the family and that he loved them."

The biker's wife and Dianne both put their hands over their chests.

"I know, isn't that so sweet? I always love it when we have a positive contact like that. Makes this all worth it," Michelle said. "Especially when you know there's not a lot of time. You see, these spirits get lost in these other planes, these multiple dimensions. I like to call it the astral lasagna, where different timelines are all merging, stacked on top of each other, and souls across the generations are all fighting to push themselves through. Sometimes, they get pushed into our plane through a symbol, and sometimes it's through a full manifestation of a ghost. You just never know what you're gonna get or how strong the spirit is.

"But either way, our job on this plane is to help push those spirits onward to their ultimate destination. We have to help them completely cross over, so they don't have to keep struggling to find the living through all those layers. It can be as simple as getting a basic 'I love you' message across or as hard as blessing an entire house with holy water. It's just the luck of the draw." She started to move around the room and gather the candles from various spots.

"Wait a minute," the biker man said. "Are we done already?"

Michelle turned from the mantel. "For tonight, yes. But we do a séance every night on these tours. You're free to come back as many times as you'd like. We get returning guests all the time. And, of course, we have those who come by once and never want anything to do with ghosts or séances ever again." She laughed as she nodded her head toward the door.

"But what about E. W.?" the guy with glasses asked.

"I'm afraid we better let E. W. be," Michelle said before she swiped some dust from beneath a photograph of the Ashfords standing in a field. "I know that was exciting and all, but...let me put it this way...that spirit was a bit negative with its energy. Kinda dark. I think that the young woman and her boyfriend were right to leave if they were scared. Sometimes if you hang around an active place too long, especially if you hold a séance, a dark spirit will try to stick to you. That's especially the case if you're very scared or negative yourself. Not that that girl was negative, but it was pretty obvious she was turned off by the whole thing."

"Right, but we ain't scared," the biker man said. His eyes widened at the rest of the group as if to tell everyone to agree with him. "Were any of you?"

The guy with glasses said, "It made me jump. Sure."

"I was a little spooked," Dianne said. "But I'm all right."

"I'm terrified," Megan added, clearly lying through her teeth. "Absolutely terrified."

The biker man blew air from his nose, disappointed. "Well, what if we tried to contact E. W. again? Just us?" He looked over at the guy with glasses, then over towards Michelle.

Michelle shook her head. "I think it's getting too dark outside, and I don't want you guys getting stuck in the rain. Besides, with those two gone, we may not have enough collective energy. Less so if we lose the two sisters here. I don't want to terrify another one." She pointed at Megan, who gave Michelle big, exaggerated nods in return.

"She's not actually scared," Dianne said, rolling her eyes at the fact Megan convinced Michelle. "My sister is messing with you. She doesn't believe in this kind of stuff. Believe me."

"Oh, is that right?" Michelle said.

Megan shook her head. The biker couple looked over at her, trying to hide their distaste at the night coming to an end.

"Yeah," Dianne said as she grabbed her sister's arm, giving it a hard squeeze. "But I think we're gonna head out, too. Thank you for a great tour. I really enjoyed it! Maybe someday I'll come back myself." She meant what she said, but since Dianne was trying to push her irritating sister out of the house, it came across as disingenuous, which was a shame considering she wanted to stay longer.

Michelle walked the Willis sisters out of the dusty, smoky living room, to the door. "Would you like some help getting back to the road?"

"We're good, but thank you," Dianne said.

Megan pretended to shiver in fright.

"How about an umbrella?" Michelle asked, peering out of the dark, water-spotted window by the door. "Looks like the rain is starting to pick up again."

Dianne and Megan declined, but both thanked Michelle for the tour before they exited the Ashford House and made their fast walk back to the Ford at the end of the graveled path. Dianne waited until they were just far enough away to start explaining to her sister how rude she was for pretending to be scared. Meanwhile, back inside the haunted house, Michelle returned to the living room to clean up and help the remaining three guests get on their way as well.

"I forgot to ask them if they wanted to buy any merch," Michelle said. "Would any of you want a T-shirt or a hoodie?" She pulled the bottom of her Ashford House shirt to show the design. "I can get them from my car if any of you are interested."

The guests looked at each other and shrugged.

"I just want to talk to another ghost," the biker man said with a chuckle. "E. W."

Michelle smiled, proud of herself that she conducted a compelling séance. "I know, and I'd hate to leave you wanting more, but I'm afraid E. W. has left the building."

"Where'd she go?" the biker's wife asked. "Who was she looking for?"

Michelle paused, thinking for a moment. "You know, in my opinion, I think E. W. must've had something to do with that poor girl who kept screaming. Her or those sisters that just left."

"You think so?" the guy with glasses asked.

Michelle nodded before she picked up the candlestick from the circular table. "I think it was a dead grandmother. A distant relative. You get those spirits sometimes. They tend to push their way through like that, but if you're not expecting it, it can be a bit too much to handle, especially if they try to attach themselves to you. The last thing anyone wants is a nasty grandma trying to visit you."

Chapter 14

The Unlocking

Dianne rocked through waves of nausea again as she returned to the nurse's station inside Wing A. The holes in the ceiling were now twice as big, spilling acrid water from above. It smelled like sewage, and it was a dark brown, almost black color that puddled on the already filthy floor. She had to cover her nose and mouth with her elbow as she headed toward the desk, trying her best to move quickly and concisely.

The two keys Dianne retrieved from Nurse Grantham were the first to come out. She had placed them in a separate pocket, away from the other keys so that she could get to them more easily. The first one was an unmarked silver key, the other a bronze with a faded WING A label on the top, a duplicate.

Dianne placed the silver key into the lock on the corner of the top drawer. It slid inside with no problem. Dianne twisted it, heard a slight click, and then pulled the drawer out to find a whole set of silver keys lined inside. Each one was labeled with a little white tag. Room numbers. They were all there in one magnificent collection. In fact, the set of keys sitting in the drawer was the most beautiful thing Dianne had seen in the decrepit hospital. Everything that surrounded her was defiled and broken, but these keys were in perfect condition somehow.

Without wasting time Dianne plucked the key for Room 222 out of the batch. She clutched it tightly in her hand as she started to run toward the stairwell at the end of the hall. Dianne had to dodge the black waterfalls and pools of putrid liquid in her speediness. One was a little deeper than she thought, and her sneakers were almost completely submerged in the filthy wetness.

Dianne elbowed open the double doors at the end of the hall, pushing puddles of water in the process. Her shoes were soaked as she traversed the dark water, heading towards the stairs.

"Oh, come on!" she cried out as she discovered the stairs were nothing but a bleak waterfall. No steps remained, only the pouring, stinking water from the second floor landing above. A steady stream fell and splashed, leaking out through the exit doors. Dianne held her elbow tight against her nose and mouth as she turned away and returned to the hallway, where she found she was no longer alone.

In the beam of Dianne's flashlight, beyond the multiple leaks from the ceiling, was a woman in a wheelchair making her way up the hall. Her face drooped with eyes almost hollow under crooked glasses. Her stomach bloated out beneath her stained shirt, and she groaned with every push of the fat wheels on either side of her chair.

"Nurse," the sickly woman said in a weak voice. "Nurse, please. Help me."

Dianne didn't respond as she moved closer. She

couldn't stop and stare since time was of the essence. She had to go around this woman and fast.

"Nurse..." The woman rolled herself underneath one of the leaks, but the dark water didn't touch her face. She stayed dry, unaffected. "It hurts so bad..."

The woman didn't flinch when Dianne shot her flashlight at her face. Much like with the doctor and Gerald Swaggart, the woman seemed blind to the brightness. However, as Dianne hugged the wall and went by the wheelchaired woman, the woman's head turned in Dianne's direction. She sensed her presence, see her through the layers of dimensions.

"Please... I can't take this much longer."

Dianne shook her head but didn't speak. Instead, she turned from the woman and kept moving toward the nurse's station and elevators, keeping a quick pace despite being unaware of how to get upstairs.

"You have to help me..." The woman groaned. Her hoarse voice echoed over the vacant, wet hallway. "My...my..."

There was a heavy thud. Dianne spun around and shined her light back down the hall to see the woman lying on the floor just before her wheelchair. The woman was unmoving for a moment, but before Dianne took her eyes off her again, she started to crawl forward at a sluggish, struggling pace.

The elevator dinged to Dianne's left, and the little bulb between the two of them stuttered until it gave off a harsh white light. The right elevator opened wide to show no one inside, as if the old thing was beckoning Dianne to step inside and take a ride.

"Please..." The woman crawled closer, picking up

speed. Her whole body was dry even though she crept through the black puddles and constant water raining down from the holes above.

With the dread building in Dianne's stomach, and her heart rate rising, she spun around to face the other end of the hallway, where her flashlight met the faces of patients peeking out of their rooms, staring back at her in an unsettling stillness.

There were men and women on either side of the hall who wore a mixture of hospital gowns and casual clothing—tattered and torn. Their faces were sunken. Eyes mad. No doorway was vacant. It seemed that the entire first floor was filled with the mentally ill, each standing with a set of twinkling eyes that glistened white in the beam of Dianne's flashlight. They were unlike any ghost she'd ever seen. They looked more like zombies than spirits—skeletons with hanging flesh instead of phantoms with translucent skin.

Dianne whipped back around to see the crawling woman was almost to her. The elevator idled. She turned back again and saw the patients shuffling out of their rooms, making their way toward her.

With a terrified yelp, Dianne forced herself to enter the dingy elevator. She clicked the faded button labeled 2 over and over again until the metal door began to shut with a rumble. Dianne backed herself up against the back of the elevator as she kept her elbow covering her mouth and nose, and her flashlight pointed ahead. Just as the metal door slid shut, she saw the crawling woman reach for her, as well as multiple hands trying to pry the door back open. The elevator sealed itself and ascended before any of the ghosts could get through.

Inside the rising pitch-black elevator, Dianne kept her

eyes shut as she breathed heavily into her sleeve. There was no music inside the sealed square, only the sounds of the slow climb. Beyond the metal walls, it sounded like the elevator was traveling through the deep sea.

A slight tremble rocked Dianne back and forth. The elevator stopped. Dianne's stomach dropped. She didn't open her eyes until she heard the familiar ding sound. The door rattled open.

Much to her surprise, her flashlight showed her the second-floor hallway. Black water spilled everywhere, and the holes doubled in size from before, but Dianne was at least happy to see that the elevator didn't take her to an entirely new place in time.

"Megan!" she shouted as she leaped out into the hall, careful not to fall into one of the several holes. "Megan, I have the key!"

Dianne gasped under her elbow as she approached Room 222 and found that black water came from all the other rooms in the hallway. A puddle formed outside of Megan's room, but it wasn't rushing like it was from the other doorways. Dianne prayed that her sister wasn't dead, drowned from the sickening sewage.

"Megan!"

The key for Room 222 remained intact in Dianne's palm. It didn't crumble to dust like so many other things in the hospital. Dianne placed the key inside the lock above the handle as the black water rushed by her shoes. Her hands shook like leaves.

"Megan, I have it unlocked! I'm coming in!"

Opening the door brought a fresh wave of sickening scents, but Dianne didn't notice as she was so eager to reunite with her sister.

"Megan!" Dianne shouted as she shined her light on her weeping sibling. Megan was crouched with her back against the wall, her head in her hands. Dianne had never seen her sister like this before, in absolute misery.

Megan shot her head up. Her eyes were wide with surprise. "Dianne!"

The sisters met halfway across the room and embraced in a tight hug as they stood in the middle of the sewage. For a moment, it seemed that the sisters weren't inside Shaded Grove anymore. As they held onto each other with tears in their eyes, all was calm in the world. The chaos was gone.

"Are you hurt?" Megan asked through her cries. "Did anyone touch you?"

Dianne shook her head against her sister's shoulder. "I'm okay. Are you all right?"

"I am, but...there...there..." Megan choked on her words. "There are pictures..."

Dianne leaned back and saw her sister visibly over-whelmed, out of her element. "C'mon, let's get out of here. This whole place is falling apart."

Megan kept mumbling about pictures as Dianne led her out of Room 222, back into the stinking, wet hallway where the black water continued to stream across the tiles and spill into the gaping holes. Dianne saw the patients below clawing at the closed elevator doors like feral animals.

"The stairs are gone," Dianne said as she held onto Megan's arm and kept her close as the two of them stood just outside of the room. "We can't use the elevators. Do you think you can jump if we go to the stairwell? I think that's our only way out."

"Dianne...," Megan whispered. "There are photos of us...pictures of us as kids.... They came from the water."

"Okay," Dianne said, more interested in escaping than

focusing on her sister's statement. "Let's just go." She went to move herself and Megan toward the stairwell door at the end of the hall to the left when a familiar voice came from Room 222.

"Leaving me already, are you?"

Dianne and Megan shot themselves around, snapping their flashlights on the withered old woman who stood in the doorway. It was her, the woman they nearly killed earlier in the night. The same woman who flew against the dashboard of the Ford when Megan veered off the road, sending the car spinning down the wooded hill.

She had her same stained and wet outfit on. The dirtied and damp sweater. Her hair was askew, and her face hung low with angered eyes that sat behind large lenses that appeared more like magnifying glasses.

"You come by to visit me, and then you try to run away," the old woman said as she stepped out into the hallway. She didn't seem to notice the dark water seeping into her fuzzy blue slippers. "How can you treat me like this? Was it your mother again? Did she tell you more lies about me? Did she try to scare you off?"

Dianne and Megan backed away from the deranged woman as they shared the same terrified sinking feeling in their stomachs. Neither of them spoke.

"Do you know how lonely it is in here? How long I've prayed to see the two of you?" The old woman shuffled forward until she hovered over one of the holes in the floor.

"We don't know you," Dianne said with a shaky voice. "I'm sorry, but you must have the wrong people."

The words struck a chord with the old woman. Her eyebrows curled, and her wrinkled fingers folded into fists. "No! I do not have the wrong people! Just because you've been hidden away by your rude and crude mother doesn't mean I can't recognize my own granddaughters!"

The sisters looked over at each other, eyes wide with the same horror and confusion they'd shared since the start of the night.

Megan returned her glare at the old woman and said, "Those pictures of us in your room. How did you get them?"

"Why, your mother, of course." The old woman's voice turned oddly calm again. It sounded more unsettling than her angered tone from a second ago. "When you're locked away in a hospital like this, miles and miles away from home, the only way I can see the two of you grow up is through photographs. And what marvelous young women you've turned out to be. I hope you're nothing like your mother, who has been nothing but cruel to me. Just look at me, look at your poor grandmother, all alone in this place."

The sisters shook their heads as they kept their lights trained on the woman.

"That's why you can't leave me. What else can I do when your mother, my only daughter, keeps you away from me all the time?"

"We're not your granddaughters," Dianne said without a shred of confidence. The night was so chaotic, so mind-bending, she wasn't sure of anything anymore. "We wouldn't even recognize you. Our mother's never mentioned—"

"Of course not!" the old woman shouted, making the sisters jump back an inch. "She's ashamed of me! Why else would she put me in here?! She hates me! She hates her mother!"

Dianne had to catch herself after her heel went over the

edge of one of the holes. Megan grabbed onto her arm, and the two of them stood still just before the door to the stairwell. Water rushed out from the doors on either side of them.

"And now that you're here, after years of being deprived of my grandchildren, you're leaving me! What do I have to do to just spend a little time with the two of you?" The old woman crept closer.

"We don't believe you," Dianne said. "You're trying to mess with us like all the other spirits here."

"Yeah, we don't want any trouble. We don't wish you any harm," Megan added. It was a surprising thing to say, considering she sounded like Michelle during the Ashford House séance, the same séance that Megan didn't even believe was real, at least not at the time.

The old woman shot her arms outwards, exposing her leathery, liver-spotted skin as they slid out from her faded pink sweater. A hospital bracelet dangled off her left wrist. She held it out toward Dianne and Megan. "Do you believe this?"

The sisters lowered their lights on the lettering of the bracelet. The name read: ETHEL K. WILLIS. It wrapped around the old woman's wrist as she held her shaking hand out for all to see.

"No," Dianne said, shaking her head. "No way."

"And you're little Dianne," Ethel said. "Dianne and her older sister, Megan. Two beautiful girls. You both look just like your mother. She was a pretty girl. It's too bad she had to grow up to disrespect her poor mother, who only did her best to raise a family all by herself. Did she ever tell you how lazy your grandfather was?"

Dianne and Megan saw other patients coming out of their rooms down the hall. Glistening eyes shined through the dark. They heard more people on either side of them, hidden somewhere around the flooded corners.

"Why won't you stay with me? Why won't you hug your poor grandmother for once? I've longed to hold you." Ethel's voice was contorted, and her mouth turned into a snarl, exposing her grayed and yellowed teeth. She shot her arms out again before she jumped forward with an unexpected speed.

Dianne and Megan took another step back when the floor crumbled before their feet. The two of them screamed and shut their eyes tight as their bodies fell through the floor. The black sewage followed, raining down on them as they fell to the first floor, where the tiles immediately crumbled under their weight, sending them down another level, into the basement of Wing A.

The sisters landed hard on an overturned gurney mattress, rolling onto the cemented floor next to it. Megan's fat flashlight flew from her hand and crashed against the wall. Its bulb erupted, extinguishing the orange glow with a loud crack.

Both Dianne and Megan were soaked and filthy from the smelly water that fell in a dark shower from the two floors above. Dianne scrambled to her feet, dry heaving between her knees as Megan clutched her arm as she remained on the ground. The sisters' skins were muddied and battered like they were just shot from a grimy cannon.

"Megan." Dianne coughed and heaved before turning to pick up her flashlight. It was still working despite the fall. "Are you okay?"

"Ah, shit!" Megan said behind gritted teeth. "My arm!" She rolled on her back.

"Let me see." Dianne knelt and shined her light on Megan's right arm. No bones stuck out from the leather jacket, but Dianne had to see if there was any damage underneath.

"Don't touch it!" Megan said before looking down at herself, her hands and legs.

"It's all right. Just relax. Can you take your jacket off?"

"Hold on, hold on. Let me catch my breath. I need a minute." Megan jerked her head to the side before Dianne brushed her dripping hair away from her face. "Thanks. Are you all right?"

"Yeah, I think so." Dianne sounded out of breath. "Don't worry about me." She turned her flashlight to the right, illuminating a hallway with more gurneys and thrown medicine bags. There were doors made of steel that had tiny square-shaped openings at their tops. "I guess we're underground now."

"Great...," Megan sighed. "That bitch..."

Through the sounds of the spilling water, Ethel's voice echoed from the holes above. "Watch your mouth, young lady. That's no way to talk."

"Shove it, old lady!" Megan shouted up at the withered voice. "You're not our grandmother!"

"Megan..." Dianne didn't want any trouble. Taunting the spirit wouldn't help the sisters in the slightest.

Ethel's voice returned, a little more somber. "So, you're not much different than your mother, after all. She used to talk to me like that, too. So disrespectful, so unaware of how much work I've done to take care of her. Yet here we are."

"If you wanna help, why don't you get us out of here?" Megan asked as she kept a tight clutch on her aching arm. Tears fell from her cheeks in dark droplets. "Why not be a real grandmother and call an ambulance for us? Can't you see we're dying in this nasty place?"

"Oh, you'll be taken care of one way or another. Don't

worry. I'll be down there soon to deal with you myself. Just you and your sister wait!" Ethel said with her anger returning.

Dianne wanted to pull her sister away from the hole and stop the back and forth, but she knew her sister was hurting. "C'mon, Megan. Ignore her."

"You can't ignore me," Ethel said, sounding farther away. "I'm a part of you, just as you are a part of me."

Chapter 15

The Basement

The depths of Wing A were as decrepit and sickening as the sisters could imagine. The walls were rotten, stained with reds and brown that streaked what must've been white at one point in time. Cracks slithered along the tarnished concrete floor. Trash littered every inch; hospital beds and half-used syringes, single metal wheels, bits of leather straps, puddles of the black water.

The sounds of the trickling sewage continued at a constant pace as Dianne and Megan slowly walked down the only hallway they could go. With a big pile of rubble blocking the way behind where they landed in the basement, the Willis sisters had to go around, venturing into the U-shaped layout of Shaded Grove Mental Hospital's underground.

Megan was able to peel her soaked leather jacket off and find her arm intact. No bones stuck out from her skin, although there was a pretty large, dark bruise starting to form just before her elbow. Despite it hurting her, Megan couldn't help but press on it with her fingers. The pain that shot through it gave her a jolt of adrenaline, keeping her more awake and alert.

"It smells even worse down here," Megan said as Dianne led her forward with her flashlight. "Do you think it's over? Do you think we're dead now?"

"No, not yet," Dianne replied. "I think if we were supposed to be dead, they would've killed us by now."

"If that fall didn't get us, I wonder just what *will*."

"At least we're together again. Better to die with each other than by ourselves, right?"

The two of them continued walking at a snail's pace. Both sisters had a slight limp.

The steel doors lined the left side of the hall, while doors labeled OFFICE and UTILITY were on their right. A big dusty window stood in between. It reflected Dianne and Megan's tattered appearances at them in the light. Neither sister wanted to investigate the rooms, especially not after they heard a faint scream coming from somewhere in the dark.

"Oh, God..." Megan had her hand over her beating chest.

Dianne covered her flashlight's beam with her hand.

"What are you doing!? I can't see!" Megan said.

"Shh, I'm trying to keep us hidden," Dianne whispered.

"From the ghosts? I'm pretty sure they can tell where we are."

"I don't know. I think it worked before."

The scream returned but didn't come closer. The way it was muffled made it sound like it was coming from behind one of the distant steel doors. It was a man's scream— guttural and terrified.

"C'mon," Dianne said, starting to move again. "We just

have to keep moving. If we stay still for too long, we may miss our chance to get out."

The hallway turned to the right, showing the sisters more steel doors and a room labeled LAB. Pounding sounds followed the man's screams as black water cascaded from the walls.

Dianne's flashlight bounced from left to right as she anticipated one of the doors opening and a maniacal ghost running out into the hallway to find them. Maybe Ethel, their so-called grandmother, or one of the many other patients roamed these floors. Dianne wasn't sure which kind of spirit would be easier to deal with.

The hallway turned to the right again, and Dianne's flashlight shined straight ahead, illuminating the two elevators at the far end, just next to the pile of blocking rubble. Without being too harsh, Dianne grabbed Megan's arm and headed toward the elevators.

"They were working when I came up to get you from the second floor. Maybe we can ride them up and go through the first-floor exit," Dianne said, trying to move as quickly as possible.

Megan didn't argue.

Beyond more steel doors and a room labeled THER-APY, the sisters approached the darkened elevator doors. No light shined from the circular bulb above, and the buttons with the upward arrows didn't glow or work. The constant pressing by Dianne didn't garner any reaction beyond the metal. As far as she could tell, the elevators were dead.

"This can't be happening," Dianne said under her breath as she tried to pull open the elevator door herself. "They were working literally a moment ago. It opened right up for me!"

Megan could only muster up so much strength to try and get the old elevator door open.

"Stop. Don't hurt your arm," Dianne said. "They obviously don't want us going this way." She turned back and faced down the hallway again, watching the opposite end from which they came. To her left stood a door to the men's bathroom that sat half-covered by the pile of rubble from above.

"So, we just have to do what they say?" Megan asked, but not in a sarcastic and insincere way. "We have no power over them?"

"We do, it's just...I'm not entirely sure how we can get through to them."

Megan sighed and placed her hand on the door of the right elevator. "This is so messed up. Like, for real."

"I know, I know." Dianne's voice was worn out.

"And what about that old lady? Ethel Willis. Did you see her bracelet?" Megan held her wrist up as if she was wearing one herself.

"Yeah..."

"Do you think she's legit?" Megan asked. "I mean, Mom barely talked about our grandparents. You weren't even born when grandma died. *I* wasn't even born when grandpa died." She paused and swiped her dripping hair out of her eyes. "I know this sounds completely bonkers, but is that lady the ghost of Mom's mom?"

Dianne didn't give her sister an answer, she just raised her eyebrows and pursed her lips.

"Like, this was where she died, and we somehow came in contact...wait...the séance... Michelle and the letters. E. W.... Ethel Willis. No way..."

Dianne nodded. "I didn't even think about that. With everything going on I totally forgot all about—"

"No, it just hit me now. I thought this whole thing was an elaborate joke, but then I saw those pictures of us in her room." Megan shook some of the dark water off her clothes. "E. W. Can you believe this?"

"I don't know what I believe," Dianne replied.

"But wait," Megan said, moving closer to her sister. "If grandma died when I was really young, and you weren't born yet, how would she even have those photos of us?"

Before Dianne registered Megan's question, she heard loud footsteps coming from down the hall.

"Shh, hold on." Dianne grabbed her sister's arm again and hid behind the corner wall next to the putrid bathroom, peeking her head around to see one of the doors on the right side of the hall open.

"Is it her? Is it Ethel?" Megan asked in a hushed voice.

"Shh," Dianne repeated as she did her best to hide the shine of her light.

Halfway up the hall, a man stepped out from the doorway and walked directly across to another room in front of him. From what Dianne could make out, the man wore a white coat and dark pants. He held some sort of device in his hands. He reminded Dianne of Dr. Gray, although she wasn't sure if it was the same doctor. After all, Dr. Gray collapsed into a cloud of dust before the entire pair of the Doctor's Quarters fell apart.

Dianne turned to her sister and said, "I think he just came from the stairs. Let's go see. C'mon, we have to be fast."

Megan didn't say a word as she let her sister guide her through the dark, toward the unlocked door where the mysterious doctor came from.

With their shoes splashing against the black water, Dianne and Megan entered the doorway to find all but two steps staring back at them. The remaining were all hidden beneath big slabs of concrete and pieces of broken brick.

"Go back," Dianne said in a whispered panic. "Go back to the elevators."

The sisters moved with frantic feet back to their corner spot as the door across from the stairwell opened again, bringing the doctor back into the hallway. Behind him, a ray of orange light spilled into the darkness for a moment, along with the scream from the tortured man and the pounding noises. Both the light and the cries of terror were muffled as the door finally shut.

With Megan behind her, Dianne crouched and squinted, seeing the doctor moving toward the left turn at the other end of the hall. Soon he was out of sight.

"It must be a doctor working on one of the patients," Dianne said.

"Where is he going?" Megan asked.

"I don't know, but I think we have to go in that room."

"What? Are you serious? I don't want to know what's going on in there. Can't you hear he's dying?" Megan's voice shook. She couldn't control her volume. "What the hell do you think we're gonna find in there?"

Dianne shook her head, trying to get her mind straight. "Remember what Michelle was saying about pushing the spirits through? How sometimes a ghost just needs a little help getting to where it needs to go in the afterlife?" She spoke quickly. "They get stuck in a loop, trapped in between."

"Yeah, I guess."

"I think we have to help them somehow. This guy screaming. There was a guy in a wheelchair from before. Gerald. Even our grandmother or whatever."

"But we helped Gerald. He screwed us over," Megan said, getting some of her anger back.

"But we didn't push him through. We didn't help him all the way."

"That guy wanted a bath! You're telling me we have to wash these crazy people!?"

Dianne started to laugh, so much so that she had to cover her mouth. It wasn't a healthy belly laugh; it was more of a nervous breakdown kind. Something about Megan's words set off a laugh that took away the last breath of Dianne's sanity, sending her into hysterics.

"Dianne, what are you doing?" Megan started laughing herself, finding her sister's behavior contagious. Her giggles mixed with Dianne's, and pretty soon, the two filthy and battered sisters were collapsing into each other as they struggled to stifle their laughter.

"This is just so ridiculous," Dianne said as tears streamed down her face. She was laughing so hard that she started to lose her breath. "Bathing an old man. What am I thinking? What is this place?"

Megan snorted and grabbed Dianne's arm as she tried to keep herself from falling to the floor.

"They should commit *us* to this place," Dianne said, gasping.

Megan continued to laugh. She nodded and said, struggling, "I'll wash your ass if you wash mine."

The sisters' laughter reignited from Megan's line, and the two of them let themselves go laughing. They didn't care how loud they were during the moment of their manic giggling. Both of their stomachs started to hurt from the laughs.

It took a few minutes for the girls to settle down. With all that the sisters endured, it would take some time for their minds and bodies to recalibrate themselves. It seemed that the longer Dianne and Megan stayed inside Shaded Grove, the deeper the ominous energy sunk its claws into their sanity, twisting their emotions around in waves of possession, not necessarily from one spirit or another, but rather the hospital as a whole. Every building, every floor, the entire premise was an entity of the dark, the lost and forgotten. The neglected and the damned.

"All right. Okay," Dianne said, letting out a final few giggles. "We have to keep moving." She grabbed her sister's face with her dirty hands, but Megan didn't flinch. "We have to go into that room, okay? Can you do that for me?"

Megan, who smiled back at Dianne with watery red eyes, replied. "Yep, whatever I have to do." Her laughter was fading, too, although she sounded stoned out of her mind. She spoke in a breathy voice.

"Okay, let's go. Stay with me." Dianne took Megan's hand and grabbed her flashlight from the floor. Together, the sisters moved up the hall with quick steps, heading toward the room with the screaming man and the orange light, the room labeled: THERAPY. Dianne swung the wooden door open and entered with Megan right behind her.

A white plastic curtain was drawn around the center of the decrepit room. An orange lamp hung above, casting a glow against the curtains, showing the sisters a silhouette of a human figure sitting up, twitching and shifting as screams escaped his mouth. All sorts of shadowed machinery surrounded him, but Dianne wasn't sure what they were at first. They looked like fat boxes with antennas, and the man's shadow appeared to be wearing headphones.

Then, the smell came. It wasn't the familiar scent of sewage that covered every inch of them. It was burnt hair.

Burnt flesh, too. It was harsh on the nose, and hot in the throat.

Dianne and Megan crept closer. Any bit of laughter that remained in the Willis sisters vanished the moment Dianne pulled the curtain aside to reveal a man with a fried scalp lying on a hospital bed. The skin on his head had circular burns, exposing fresh flesh beneath. The shadowed headphones turned out to be a plastic band that sat on the man's burnt hair. Two fat cotton balls wrapped in gauze were on either end, hanging just before his temples.

"P-please, d-don't do it!" the man cried to the sisters. "Don't hurt me again. I-I can't take it! Please!" His eyes were wide, white, and terrified beneath the orange lamp above.

"We're not going to hurt you," Dianne said, lowering her flashlight. She took in the scene for a moment. The burnt patient. His sweat-stained shirt. The leather straps that not only constrained his wrists and feet but his chest, too. The radio-like machines beside his bed. Everything was vintage, outdated.

"Oh, God. Jesus in Heaven," the man said, convulsing. "Let me out! Let me out!"

Megan glanced behind her, looking out for the doctor. She didn't pull the curtain back all the way.

"Just calm down, sir. We're going to do our best to help you, okay?" Dianne said. She approached the right side of the bed and motioned Megan to the other side. Dianne saw that the man's wrists were blistered and bloodied from rubbing against the tight leather.

"Oh, God. God in Heaven. Mary and Joseph." The man went on.

"We should do this quick," Megan said as she started on

the man's ankle strap. "I think that doctor will be back soon."

"Right," Dianne replied before the man continued to whine.

"No, please, not the doctor! No more doctors, I can't take it anymore! The nurses! Oh, God! Oh, Jesus!"

Through their trembling fingers, Dianne and Megan got both ankle straps off in decent time, however, the bed started to shake as the man flailed his pale legs around.

"Shh, shh. Stop that," Dianne said, trying to calm the man down. "We're not going to hurt you. We're here to help."

The man relaxed his feet a little, allowing the sisters to work on his wrists.

"That's better," Megan said.

The man breathed heavily. "They-they wouldn't stop. They were trying to kill me!"

Faint footsteps echoed behind the curtain and beyond the doorway. Voices.

"Tried to burn me alive, the devils! Oh, please get me out of here! I don't want them to turn the machine on again. It hurts so bad." He started to weep.

"Hold on. We almost have you," Dianne said. She and Megan were finishing up with the wrist straps and were about to go for the final chest buckle when the therapy room door swung open. Multiple voices came booming in. Men and women. Each of them was calling out from beyond the closed curtain as they came closer.

"We shouldn't have left him alone," a male voice said.

Dianne and Megan let go of the chest piece as the man wiggled on the bed, reaching out for the girls with his bloodied hands.

"Don't leave me!" he shouted. "Please!"

The sisters moved behind the machinery, almost tripping over the bundles of thick wires as they hid on the other side of the curtain. Dianne turned off her flashlight just before the group of people entered the front curtains and surrounded the burnt man.

"Grab his legs!" the doctor shouted. "One of you, get the guards!"

The shadows danced through the pale curtain as Dianne and Megan stood with their backs against the chilly wall. The burnt man screamed and writhed, trying to fight back against the staff.

"Who unstrapped him?" the doctor asked.

"Here, doctor," one of the nurses said, handing over a large syringe.

"Wait! His legs!" the doctor shouted. "Where is security? This is unacceptable!"

"I don't know how much longer I can keep his feet down," another nurse cried.

Dianne and Megan didn't move, and there was no telling how long they had been holding their breath. All they could do was watch the shadowed wrestling play out before their anxious eyes.

The door swung open again. Heavy footsteps entered. Keys jangled before the front curtain was pulled aside, bringing two large shadows into the scene.

"His legs," the doctor said. "He's gotten himself undone."

The burnt man screeched as the shadowed security guards did their duty, using their heavy hands to keep the patient down as the doctor attempted to administer the shot.

"Mr. Duncan, if you could just lay back and relax, this

will be over in a moment," one of the nurses said with pain in her voice.

The leather straps were being refastened as the doctor leaned down. Dianne and Megan saw the needle of the fat syringe merging with Mr. Duncan's shoulder. Pretty soon, the struggling subsided, and Mr. Duncan's shouts faded into tired gibberish until he fell silent.

The doctor blew stressed air from his mouth and said, "All right. Thank you all for your assistance. I think we should proceed with the treatment before we start pointing fingers. Does that sound acceptable?"

The shadows nodded.

"Okay. No one leaves this room until we've completed the process," the doctor said. "For everyone's safety."

The shadows nodded again.

"I'm going to start up the power. Make sure his mouth-piece is in properly this time. Keep the nodules leveled on the sides of his head, please. We cannot afford to screw this up again. I can still smell the damage, for Christ's sake."

There was movement. A flick of a switch followed by a humming sound that grew louder by the second, turning to a continuous buzz.

"Dianne," Megan whispered. She nudged her sister in the elbow.

Dianne looked over and saw Megan pointing at some-thing to the left of where she was standing. She followed her finger with panicking eyes until she realized Megan was trying to place her attention on the outlet on the wall. The thick wires from the machines snaked on the floor until they reached two plugs inserted into the outlet.

"Pull them out," Megan whispered. "Hurry."

The buzz grew louder. Dianne handed her flashlight to Megan and shuffled herself sideways until she crouched before the plugs. They were large and rectangular. She was hesitant at first, thinking that she'd be electrocuted if she made contact, but when Dianne heard the doctor about to initiate the shock therapy, she placed her hands on both plugs and pulled with all her might.

Both plugs popped from the sockets with an audible *fwunk*. Dianne fell back, and the loud buzzing sound ceased. The volume of the machines lowered as they powered down. All that remained was the orange glow of the lamp above the hospital bed that showed the multiple shadows beyond the curtains.

"What's happening to the generator? Why's everything shut off?" the doctor asked.

No one answered as the machines fell silent. The humming buzz of electricity ended.

"What in God's name is going on here?" the doctor said impatiently. "This is getting completely out of control!" He clicked and turned the knobs on the control board but found no results. He flipped switches up and down with no success. "Jesus Christ, do I have to do everything in this place? Where the hell is this thing supposed to be plugged in?"

The backside of the curtains was yanked to the side. Megan tried to get out of the way, but as the doctor stepped through, the two of them locked eyes. She saw two nurses and two security guards standing around Mr. Duncan's bed. Each of them was a faded, dated-looking man and woman who looked like they were dressed up in a 1950s-period piece production. One of which was Todd, the security guard from earlier in the night.

"Hey! Who are you? How did you get in here?" the doctor asked the sisters. He towered over the two of them, and his coat was long and dirtied, just like his worn face that drooped with sagging skin and sunken, dark eyes.

Megan hugged the wall and pushed herself to the side of the doctor so she could help Dianne up from the floor.

"Stop! Stay right there!" the doctor commanded.

Dianne sprung up. She and Megan ran around the curtains until they found the door that led them back into the hallway. Megan had to fumble with the flashlight before she found the button to turn it back on.

The doctor was right behind them, and as the sisters were about to get away, he grabbed Megan's shoulder.

"You're in a lot of trouble," the doctor said. "Guards!"

Megan spun around and smashed her flashlight into the side of his head, making it explode into a thick, hazy cloud of dark dust that instantly blinded her. Much like with Gerald Swaggart, the doctor's entire body burst into filthy particles.

"C'mon," Dianne said as she grabbed Megan's arm, pulling her down the hall toward the turn that would wrap back around to where they fell from.

Megan coughed and waved her hand before her face. Her eyes stung. Her throat dried like a desert. It didn't help that she was still wet from the fall through the floors as all the dust particles clung to her.

As the sisters sprinted and scrambled down the hall, the sound of the security guards' heavy boots echoed behind them. Dianne had to keep yanking Megan along so she wouldn't fall behind.

"Give me the light!" Dianne said.

Megan handed it over.

Now on the other side of the basement floor, moving along the steel doors and the utility and office rooms, Dianne shot the flashlight all along the putrid, flooding hall, trying to find anywhere for the two of them to hide.

Megan coughed, choking on the nasty dusting in her mouth.

The footsteps behind them came closer.

"Shit," Dianne said. Her light landed on two overturned mattresses. There were stretchers on either side, making a fort-like formation against the left wall. There looked to be enough space for someone to crawl inside. Not that it was such an alluring place to be, it was merely the only option the girls had, considering there could be spirits lurking behind any of the closed doors.

Dianne yanked Megan forward, making her yelp.

"Ouch! You're hurting my arm!" Megan cried before the dust choked her again. "Where are we going?"

"On the floor. We're gonna hide under here," Dianne said before she got down on her knees. "C'mon!"

"I can't see!"

Dianne pulled her sister down to the soaked cement floor. She got behind her and pushed her back into the mattress cave ahead of them.

"What are you doing? It's wet! My knees are soaked!" Megan complained.

"Shut up and move!"

The footsteps rounded the corner of the hall as Dianne squeezed herself backward under the beds and stretchers, making her sister's head push against the wall. The front of Dianne's shirt and pants were soaked, sitting directly in a puddle of the black water. She clicked off the flashlight and shooshed her sister's coughs once more until the sounds of the guards' voices came from just outside the mattress fort.

"Where did they go?" the one said.

"There were two of them, right?" the other asked.

"I think so. Todd, you think they were patients?"

"Let's hope not."

The one guard sighed. "We better lockdown to be safe. If two got out, that means there could be more. Dammit, what a mess. The last thing we need is a prison break around here. I wonder what the hell is going on with the power."

"Just one thing after another," Todd said. "Never a dull moment."

The guards turned back, walking down the hallway toward the utility and office rooms. Dianne covered her mouth while Megan stayed still, shoved into the corner, trying not to throw up.

"Yeah, it won't be a dull moment if we can't get a grip on the situation," the other guard said. "There's something going on here. Something's not right."

The two of them stepped into the room next to the murky window. Their voices became muffled until the only sounds that remained were the trickling waterfalls of dark water and the Willis sisters' heavy-beating hearts.

Chapter 16

The Visit

There was no sense of time inside Shaded Grove Mental Hospital, let alone the basement level. It was a constant dark, a continuous bleak night with no sense of the sun ever shining again. Every moment flew by and stayed stuck in one place at the same time. The past bled into the present, and the future was a deep mystery, seeming to change with every shift of the dimensions.

Dianne and Megan remained under their tarnished mattress fort as they waited for the next spirit, the next paranormal problem that would present itself to them.

But how much longer could they last?

Although their noses were adjusted somewhat to the stench, their bodies remained battered and bruised. The sisters felt aches on every edge of their bones, and lying contorted like pretzels beneath the stack of beds wasn't helping the fact.

"Are they gone?" Megan asked with her forehead pressed against the concrete wall.

"They went into a room. I can't see them," Dianne answered. "I can't hear anything."

"We can take them," Megan said before she coughed up a ball of dust. She gagged but held her vomit down. "This is so disgusting. I'm gonna puke any second!"

"Don't be so loud."

Megan spat onto the floor and shifted her body, causing her right boot to dig into Dianne's armpit. "Listen to me."

"What?"

"We can take these ghosts, or demons, whatever they are. They're all made of dust," Megan said, trying to wiggle her way around her sister. "If I can get out, I can just keep punching them. Then we won't have any problems and can escape this place once and for all."

"But how? We keep having to run. We keep having to hide." Dianne wasn't ready to leave the fort yet. She kept clicking her flashlight on and off to see if anyone was coming for them.

"We don't have to hide if they're all gone. Maybe we have to fight back a little more, not let them scare us so much."

"Yeah, easier said than done. We both almost died from getting all this dust in our lungs," Dianne said, sounding like her sister. "Ghosts or not, they're still scary. It's like I'm never prepared for them." Dianne sighed and wiped her hair out of her eyes. "Even if we finished them all off, where would we go?"

Megan didn't answer.

"Do you think anyone's looking for us by now? I mean, they must be, right? Mom's probably called the cops or something. Gage is probably blowing up your phone, wondering where you are," Dianne said. "I feel like we've been in here forever."

"I hope we helped that guy," Megan said. "The guy in that room with the burnt head. I wonder if they plugged in the machine again and shocked him or whatever."

"Yeah, good call on that. I hope we helped him, too. But you know what? Honestly, I'm not sure of anything anymore; if we're helping or if we're hurting. I don't know what we're supposed to do here. I thought I did, but we're just running in circles, hitting obstacle after obstacle." Dianne's tone was dipped in depression.

"I can tell you this," Megan said, "I sure wish I could punch that old lady right in the head. Maybe *that's* what we're supposed to do. Knock our so-called grandmother's lights out. She started all this." She laughed a little before the coughs took over again. "And now look where we are. I should've taken care of her when I had the chance."

Dianne thought for a moment. What her sister just said may have been the most useful statement of the entire night.

She started all this.

The night went off the rails when the sisters almost ran over the old woman in the rain. Ethel Willis. She was mental, out of her mind, demanding to be taken back to her room. When Dianne and Megan tried to help, at least what they thought was helping, Ethel exploded in a rage that caused the car to slide off the road and flip down the hillside, leading the sisters to limp through the dark woods until they discovered the mental hospital.

"We're here because she brought us here," Dianne said to herself.

"What did you say?" Megan asked.

Dianne spoke up and said, "Ethel Willis brought us here. She flipped out in the car because we must've been taking her away from the hospital. She needed to come back here, and she wanted us to go with her. That's why we survived the crash, that's why her spirit is still active in this place. She wants us. Her grandchildren, or whoever we are to her. Her energy attached itself onto us."

"And how did that happen?" Megan paused. "That séance, right? How could I forget so soon? Michelle and E. W. Just great."

"Right, and now the spirit wants something from us."

"Okay, and what do you think that is? I'll gladly give it to her."

"I don't know, but if there *is* a way out of here, it has to be through her. I can feel it."

"Oh yeah?"

"That's the only idea I have left. Helping the spirits may help them move on into the afterlife, but helping Ethel will be our ticket out of here."

Without much more being said, Dianne crawled out from the filthy bed fort on the basement floor. More black water soaked through her shirt. When she was fully out, she clicked on the flashlight to make sure the area was secure. For the moment, there were no signs of the guards, the doctor, or any of the nurses. Everything was just as it was after Todd and the other mysterious security man walked into the room just up ahead.

"Where are we going?" Megan asked as she shimmied her way out of the mattresses. When Dianne turned to shine her light on her sister, she saw Megan covered in a fine layer of gray dust. Her black hair was covered in the stuff, making her look like an older woman.

Dianne shrugged. "I guess we will check out these rooms. I heard those guards talk about the power supply and then went in..." She moved up the hall a bit until she saw the room labeled: UTILITY. "Here. I think this is where they went."

The beam of the flashlight barely penetrated through the glass of the window beside the door. Much like Megan, every inch of the thing was covered in either dust or cobwebs. Dianne tried putting her face up against the window to peer inside with her hands just above her head, but she couldn't make out much. Only a tiny red light in the corner and some sort of box against the wall.

"It could be something, could be nothing," Dianne said. "But those guys went in here for a reason."

Megan stood up straight and cracked her back. She turned her neck to the left, then right, giving her a somewhat satisfying *pop!* She wiggled her feet and brushed off what dust and water she could from her body. Droplets of dark sewage dripped off her boots and the zipper of her jacket. "You lead the way. I'm too dirty and sore to make up my mind right now."

Finding a door unlocked would've been exciting for the sisters earlier in the night, but not now. Instead of basking in the delight that there were no keys to find or alternative routes to take, Dianne and Megan pushed the wooden door open and stepped inside without missing a beat.

They let the door shut behind them.

There wasn't much room inside as metal shelves lined either side. Broken cardboard and spilled pamphlets littered the floor. Dead bugs. Cobwebs in the corners. Straight ahead were multiple fuse boxes on the wall. Long, gray pieces of metal covered each one. There were red levers, too. Each box had one below them.

In the right corner, at the end of the line of fuse boxes, was the tiny red light that Dianne saw through the cloudy window. She approached it and saw that there was a small message reading LOCKDOWN/OFF just beneath it on a white placard. Above it was an unlit bulb of the same size. The words FULL POWER were typed on a similar placard nearby.

"Maybe we can get the power back, get the elevators working again," Dianne said as she moved her light around the fuse boxes.

"Do we just pull those switches?" Megan asked.

"Looks like it."

Dianne started with the box closest to the right light. She pressed her palm on the end of the red lever and pushed it to the right. It didn't budge at first, but after Dianne applied as much pressure as she could, the lever moved over with a *clunk*. The metal door on the fuse box popped open, making Dianne jump as it made a loud snapping sound.

"Looks like the electrical box in our basement," Megan said, looking inside at the exposed switches. They were small and black, lined in two columns in the box. Torn pieces of tape with remnants of words written in marker stuck to the side. "I think they just click on like this."

With Dianne holding the light as steady as she could with her shaky hands, Megan stuck her fingers inside the black switches and pulled them to the sides. She went down the column, powering on whatever the wiring led to, and once she finished with it, the tiny red light began to blink.

"Let's hope these other two work," Dianne said. She aimed the light at the fuse box in the middle and pushed its red lever. The door snapped open. Megan switched the buttons. Somewhere, a faint noise of rattling sounded— clicking sounds. Something moved up above.

"Seems to be," Megan said.

Suddenly, a knock came against the window. It made

the sisters jump. They both spun around from the wall of fuses to see a figure standing beyond the dusty glass. The being's features were obscured. Dianne's flashlight didn't give the sisters much help.

"Are you ready to talk to me?" a voice asked from the other side of the window. It was muffled but recognizable. Ethel Willis was back. "Are you ready to behave for your grandmother?"

Megan blew irritated air from her mouth. "Great, it's her again. That old piece of..." She went straight toward the window and was about to mash her fists against the glass when Dianne stopped her.

"Wait! Don't do it, Megan," Dianne pleaded. "We need her."

"Oh, how nice of you to say, dear," Ethel said. "You know, I need the two of you, too. I've needed you for so long."

The sisters both stood before the window, taking in the shadowed figure of their ghostly grandmother. They couldn't see her facial features, only a blackened outline of her hair and small body frame.

"You have to let us out of here right now!" Megan demanded. "Or I swear to God, I'll—"

"Megan, that's enough!" Dianne shouted. Her voice was hoarse. "That's no way to talk to our grandmother!"

The shadow of Ethel shifted slightly outside. "Little Dianne, how nice of you to say that. I haven't had anyone stick up for me in, oh, well, all of my life. But I will have you know, your older sister reminds me a whole lot of my daughter, your mother, Deborah. She had the same attitude and used the same language when she spoke to me. So rude. So disrespectful."

Megan's body tensed up. Dianne moved closer, edging

her sister away from the window. She didn't want to trigger Megan, but she had to take control of the situation. If Megan got into one of her rages, there would be no chance of getting out alive.

"I know. She can be a little aggressive at times. I'm sorry about that, Grandma," Dianne said, feigning sincerity. "She's just afraid. I am, too. This place has really shaken us up. We're so tired and dirty. Is there anything you can do to help us get back home?"

Ethel's shadow stood motionless for a moment. Dianne felt her sister's impatience radiating off her, but Megan didn't move or say anything in the gap of silence.

"You want to go home so soon? Haven't you come to visit me?" Ethel said, finally. "I know you didn't come all this way just to turn around."

"You're absolutely right, Grandma," Dianne said, almost laughing at herself. She was talking to the ghost of Ethel Willis as if she were a child. "We don't want to leave here just yet. We wanted to spend some time with you if that's okay."

"Yes, yes! That would be more than okay. Oh, Dianne, that's all I ever wanted!" Ethel's shadow didn't move much. When she spoke, it was like a black-painted figure speaking. "I'd love nothing more than to see my beautiful, young granddaughters after all these years of being deprived of them. I would hate to have your mother take you away from me again. Do you think the both of you could stay for a little while?"

"Absolutely," Dianne answered. "Anything you want, Grandma."

"Oh, marvelous! And I hope Megan will want to join us, too. I know she's been difficult with her tantrums and whatnot, but I'd hate to see one granddaughter without the other."

Dianne looked over at Megan, who stood with her arms crossed.

In order to progress the back and forth with Ethel, Dianne said, "Megan would love to come with us. Right, Megan?" She gave her sister a nudge on the shoulder, making her wince in pain.

"Ow! Yes...yes," Megan whined as she rubbed up and down her bruised arm. "I'd love to spend some time with you...Grandma...."

"Oh, wonderful! I'm so happy you girls have come around," Ethel said. "But you know what, this place isn't the most pleasant place to host my granddaughters, so would you want to meet me back in my room? I can go quickly tidy it up. I'd be able to get a better look at the two of you up there."

"Room 222, right?" Dianne said, already knowing the answer.

"That's right. How sweet of you to remember," Ethel said. Her shadow slid from the window, hovering out of sight as her voice began to fade. "I can't wait to finally spend some time with you girls. I've waited so long..."

The sisters were alone now, standing before the dirty window. There were no more voices, no sounds coming from the ghost of Ethel Willis. All was quiet. Dark. Lonesome. Dianne and Megan turned around to finish their job of turning on the final of the three fuse boxes on the wall. The tiny red light kept its constant blinking in the corner.

"How are we going to get back to the second floor?" Megan asked. "There's probably nothing left up there."

Dianne shrugged and then pushed the final red lever beneath the third fuse box. "Something has to happen one way or another. All we can do is keep going. As long as we're alive, we can't give up."

"What if that crazy old lady kills us?" Megan asked. "You saw what she did to us before we fell down here. She turned into a demon. Did you see how her face changed all of a sudden?"

"That's because we resisted her," Dianne answered.

"Whatever." Megan opened the final box and began clicking the switches to their sides. With every click, the faint noises of lights and machines grew louder. The electrical current buzzed somewhere above. Gears shifted. The inner workings of Wing A woke up, yawning like a beast rising from its slumber.

When Megan reached the final two switches and snapped them to the right, the entire room filled with a flash of blinding white. The sisters each let out a little scream. Neither Dianne nor Megan could see anything before them.

"Dianne?" Megan said.

"I'm here. What's going on?" Dianne croaked out.

The whiteness lingered for a little longer until the blinding shade began to fade away, bringing the sisters' vision back. Slowly but surely, Dianne and Megan saw each other standing before the fuse boxes just as they were, only this time the room wasn't covered in dead bugs and dust. The walls weren't rotten and stained with mysterious substances. Instead, the sisters saw they were in a well-lit, properly painted room. Although the cement floor remained, it was clean from the decay. There were no cobwebs or spilled IV bags. Everything looked to be in like-new condition. Even the window by the door was new with glass that was clear enough to see through to the totally transformed hallway.

Dianne and Megan looked down at their hands, their bodies. They were still wet, filthy from the night. Their black hair still hung heavy, covered in the dust and black water. Despite the massive changes in the room around them, nothing was different in their appearances. They were as battered as they had been.

"What did we just do?" Megan asked as she looked over at the fuse boxes. The light in the corner was a stable green, lit up beside the FULL POWER placard. She glanced over at Dianne with widened eyes.

"I don't know, but whatever it was, it sent us somewhere a whole lot cleaner." Dianne clicked off her flashlight and approached the window, leaning around to look outside into the hallway at every angle. "It's all different now. Look."

Megan stood right beside her sister, seeing the fluorescent lights above that shined down on the hallway where the walls were painted a plain white. The steel doors were still across the hall, but they weren't rusted. No splatters of blood or strange brown marks. "You think it's safe to go out there?"

Dianne chuckled nervously. "Looks a lot safer than it did a second ago."

"There could be people out there," Megan said.

The sisters waited for a moment, listening. All they heard were the faint buzzing of the fluorescent lights—the slight hum of the electrical boxes behind them.

"I'd rather see ghosts in the light than the dark," Dianne said, moving to the door. "C'mon, we have to go to Ethel's room."

"You think it's just gonna be that easy?" Megan asked.

"Maybe, maybe not." Dianne opened the door. It didn't squeak on its hinges. "But we better move while we have the basement looking like this. We should go check the elevators or the stairwell."

Megan followed her sister into the hallway. There were no overturned beds, no puddles of muck. Not even the sounds of patients' screams echoed in the hall. Instead, there was an eerie quiet. It seemed the sisters were alone in the newly refreshed basement as no nurses or doctors made themselves known as Dianne and Megan went down the hall, passing by where the giant hole used to be in the ceiling. There was also no blockade of rubble preventing them from rounding the corner and approaching the elevator doors, which stood with polished metal among the white walls.

Everything was too prim and trimmed for the sisters. When they glanced back down the hall toward where the therapy room was, they saw no grime, no twisted doctors or nurses. Todd and the other security guard were nowhere to be found. The bright, quiet contrast of the dark, loud hell unsettled them. Although it was all seemingly squeaky clean for the moment, Dianne felt uneasy, like something waited for them, ready to pounce any second. She didn't feel fully alone. A presence lingered over the air.

The bulb between the elevator doors was alight, as well as the arrow buttons. Dianne pressed the up arrow. The left-side elevator opened up. The inside was empty. A single light shined from above. Music played from a tiny speaker. It sounded vintage, similar to the record that played in the doctors' quarters.

You don't remember me, but I remember you. Was not so long ago, you broke my heart in two. Tears on my pillow. Pain in my heart caused by you...

"What do you think? Should we take it up?" Dianne asked.

Megan raised her hands and said, "Do I have a choice? It's not like I have any other ideas at this point. It looks safe enough, I guess. Ouch..." She kept her right arm raised too long, causing a jolt of pain to shoot up her bones. Megan rubbed it and kept it close to her side. "Let's just get this over with."

The sisters entered the small elevator. Dianne pressed the button labeled 2 on the panel. With ease, the door slid shut. A little *bing* sounded overhead, and the elevator ascended.

If we could start anew, I wouldn't hesitate. I'd gladly take you back...

"I still can't believe all this," Megan said as she stared at the metal tiles of the elevator. Her black hair hung down, covering her face. "Absolutely insane."

Dianne couldn't disagree, but she found herself unable to respond. Like her sister, she just stared, thinking about what their grandmother would say and do to them once they returned to the second-floor room.

"What if we're the ones who are dead?" Megan asked. "And we just don't know it yet."

The elevator came to a halt. It *binged* again before the door slid open to the side. Dianne and Megan stepped out into the second floor of Wing A to a surprising sight of the floor back intact. Bright fluorescents lined the ceiling. Instead of puddles of dark water, potted plants stood on the corners. There was no trash. No leaks. No holes. No graffiti with satanic symbols and filthy imagery. Nothing like that remained, only a clean hallway with shined linoleum floors that the sisters could see their reflections in.

As the sisters moved down the hall, heading toward Room 222, they weren't being attacked by the harsh smells of black sewage water. The nasty odors were replaced by the scent of cleaning chemicals. There was also a slight humidity in the air. A hazy warm that hung like a fog that was invisible to the human eye.

They glanced across the hall at Room 221, Gerald Swaggart's room. The same room where the sisters got separated after Megan tried to stop the restless spirit in the hallway, causing the door to slam shut and lock Dianne inside. The back and forth with Gerald also caused Megan to fall into the infamous Room 222, where she was stuck behind the solid wood. Now the sisters were back, ready to re-enter the room and find out what their ghostly grandmother wanted from them.

Dianne went to knock on the door when Megan pushed her to the side and knocked on the wood herself. There were no words exchanged, but it was clear to Dianne that Megan wanted to be the typical older, protective sister. She wanted to go in first in case of any paranormal danger.

Slow footsteps approached from the other side of the door until it swung open. Ethel Willis stood smiling in the doorway, her entire body dried with unstained clothes and unmatted hair. Her thick glasses weren't cracked either. She was the picture portrait of a grandmother, small and innocent. Kind and tender.

"Hello! It's so great to see my two beautiful granddaughters," Ethel said, smiling. Behind her was a ray of sunshine beaming through the window. The kind of sunshine you saw in the late evening when the sun was just above the horizon, making long shadows on the earth and dust float inside. "What a delight it is to see you both. Please, come in, come in."

Ethel Willis' room looked more like a hotel room than a place for a mental patient. There was a made bed with pink and white sheets, a lamp on an end table, an oak dresser against the wall, and a small table in the corner with two folding chairs. Everything was wiped down and sanitized, even the bathroom, which was once the origin of the black sewage water, was a sparkling white with no signs of dark gunk ever flowing from beneath the toilet bowl.

Much like the hallway outside, the entire room sat in a humid haze. A chemical smell swirled in the air. Disinfectant. It smelled like the janitor had just mopped the floor with something strong.

"Have a seat at the table there," Ethel said as she shuffled toward the end of her bed. She took a seat in the middle of the sunlight. "I have so much to tell you and so much to ask about. Goodness, I don't know where to even start!"

The sisters crossed the room. Their shoes dripped and stained the white linoleum floor. Ethel didn't seem to notice Dianne and Megan were filthy and battered. She just smiled a big grayed-teeth smile as they sat on either side of the tiny table.

"So wonderful to have guests. You know, it's been so lonesome here. No one ever comes by, it seems," Ethel said. "But none of that matters now. You two are finally here with me. Dianne and Megan. My wonderful granddaughters."

"It's great to see you," Dianne said. She looked over at Megan, who took the sight of the clean old woman. The last the two of them saw Ethel this close up, she was drenched, standing in the street, flailing around.

"Just to be sure," Ethel said, glancing over at the door. "Your mother didn't come with you, did she?"

"No, it's just us," Dianne said. "She's back at home."

Ethel smiled again. "Oh, good. I know it's rude not to include Deborah, but I was worried she would come with you and not allow us to have enough time together. She's been awfully protective of you two."

"Why is that, Grandma?" Dianne asked. Of course, she had to keep referring to Ethel Willis as Grandma, whether it felt natural or not. Dianne had to play into the spirit's desires. She had to put herself and Megan into Ethel's world.

"Well, you know, it's just one of those things, I guess. Sometimes family members don't always see eye to eye. Not all mothers and daughters understand one another." The stream of late sunlight hit the left side of Ethel's face as she stared off into the distance for a moment. She didn't seem to mind the bright light against her eyes as she didn't blink or squint.

Dianne stared at the old woman, taking in her features. The more she looked, the more she started to see little similarities. The dark eyes. The way her eyebrows set. Through the wrinkles, she found a woman who could be related to them—a woman from another time and place.

"But we don't have to talk about all that right now," Ethel said. "I want to know all about you two." Her eyes popped, and she suddenly stood up from the edge of the bed. "I've only ever gotten to see you through photographs."

Ethel went over to the dresser and pulled out one of the bottom drawers. She moved with the pace of a shuffling snail. Her hands shook, and her legs wobbled. Dianne thought she should be using a cane or a walker, but Dianne didn't speak or try to help the old woman as she bent over to fetch the pictures.

"Your mother was at least kind enough to bring me these during her visits." Ethel brought the photos over to the table. They were the same ones Megan saw float up from the dark water. Dianne and Megan playing as young children. Birthdays. Events from early elementary school. They were all too terrifyingly specific for the sisters to appreciate. Neither of them touched the pictures.

"That's us," Megan said with her arms crossed.

"Yes, and you're both more beautiful in person!" Ethel said before returning to the edge of the bed and sitting down in the sunlight again. "Now, tell me. How old are you two now?"

Dianne answered and answered some more as Ethel kept rattling questions off. Where they went to school. If they had boyfriends. Although she was the younger of the two, Dianne was in charge of telling the story of the sisters and trying to keep Ethel from getting overwhelmed with the overload of information.

It was strange, the whole conversation, the hours that seemed to be passing. Dianne told her and Megan's life story to the spirit of their long-lost grandmother. The ghost was either their actual grandmother or another entity disguising itself as such. Dianne once learned that spirits could pretend to be someone else in order to manipulate the living. She found it happened quite often when people used Ouija boards. The users would make contact with what seemed to be an innocent spirit of a little boy or girl when in reality, it was a demon or dark entity toying with them from the other side, earning their trust so they could sneak into their souls to possess them.

Was that Ethel Willis' goal, to possess the souls of Dianne and Megan? Was she a devil in disguise? Then again, is it even possible for a single spirit to possess two people at once? If not, which one was she looking to attach herself to?

"That sounds wonderful! I'm so proud of you," Ethel said after Dianne finished telling her about being halfway through high school and Megan's experience with waiting tables. "And I'm proud of you, too, Megan. You must meet quite a cast of characters every night."

"Yeah," Megan said. "Quite the cast..." She looked at Ethel in a way that said, *And you're the biggest character of them all!*

"It's so great to hear my granddaughters are making their way in the world. Such mature young ladies you've turned out to be," Ethel said. She gave the two of them a big, toothy smile. "Just lovely."

The sisters nodded, smiling back at the old woman.

"But we'd love to hear about you," Dianne said before glancing at Megan. "Wouldn't we?"

"Yes, tell us all about you, Grandma. What stories can you tell us?" Megan asked, giving her best impression of interest. Her arms remained crossed against her chest.

Ethel raised her wrinkled, liver-spotted hands and said, "Oh, there's not enough time in the world to talk about little old me. It'd put the two of you to sleep."

"I don't think so," Dianne said. She looked over at her sister, who was trained on Ethel with impatient eyes. Then, Dianne glanced down at the photographs on the table. The one on top was her and Megan playing outside in the grass when they were both under the age of six. "Why don't you tell us about when you were a little girl?"

A weak chuckle came out of Ethel's mouth. "That was a long time ago." She paused and then turned her head toward the window, letting the sunlight hit her directly in the face. Ethel didn't squint from the brightness. "I don't know if I can remember enough."

In the spotlight of the setting sun, Ethel looked translucent. The rays of light hit her skin, going through her aged body the way a drawn curtain would glow from the light outside. If the sun were any brighter, Ethel would fade away.

"What about your parents?" Dianne asked. "Our great-grandparents. What were they like?"

Ethel turned her head away from the window in an eerie slowness and faced the sisters. "My parents? My mother and father?"

Dianne nodded. Megan stared.

A frown replaced the normal smile on Ethel's face. Her eyebrows curled. It wasn't the angered snarl like the sisters saw before they fell through the floors, but a pain, a saddened pain.

"Oh, Grandma," Dianne said, "you don't have to—"

"My mother and father were...not the easiest on me." Ethel's whole demeanor changed. She spoke as if all the air was coming out of her body. "But they did what they thought was best, I suppose."

"That's okay. Why don't you tell us how you met Grandpa instead," Dianne said, trying to change the subject so the spirit wouldn't get upset. But Ethel didn't acknowledge what Dianne had requested.

"Have you ever known someone who didn't seem to listen? Someone who, no matter how hard you tried, you couldn't get through to?" Ethel asked.

In a burst of nervous laughter, Dianne replied, "Sure, sounds like Megan to me." She looked over to her sister, hoping to get her laughing to maybe ease the tension of the situation.

No luck. Megan remained stone-faced.

"Oh, oh, no. I hope she doesn't turn out just like him." Ethel placed her skeletal hands over her eyes. "I can still see my father standing in the doorway of my bedroom, angrier than the Devil, shouting at the top of his lungs at me even though I didn't do anything wrong. He would do that to me a lot, have a sudden change in his mood. Like flipping a switch, he'd go from unbothered to a red, red rage."

The sisters didn't speak.

"Ethel, you've been a very bad girl!" Ethel's voice was low, deeper. "Now, if you don't come out here, you'll get double the usual spanks! Don't make me come in there and drag you out!" Her voice shifted back to normal. "And I would cry and cry, begging for my mother to stop him. But she never did."

The sisters froze in their seats, unsure how to react to their grandmother's sudden, dramatic shift. Just a moment ago, Ethel smiled ear-to-ear as she listened to the tales of Dianne and Megan's life stories. Now she was close to tears and refusing to stop reliving her childhood trauma.

"And I'd go out there," Ethel continued, "hoping to get the lesser side of the punishment, but he'd still give me double anyway. I'd get a spanking until I was sore all over!"

Dianne tried to stop the painful reminiscing but couldn't. No matter what she said, Ethel carried on.

"No matter how much I tried to stop, no matter how much I begged, he never let up. And this happened again and again. Whether I was well behaved or made a simple mistake, I'd get the same punishment!"

Dianne attempted to interject. "Why don't we—"

"They have no idea how sad of a child I was, how lonesome and afraid I was. All I wanted was someone to love me, someone to hold me without hurting me."

Ethel's words struck the sisters, especially Megan. Tears spilled down her murky cheeks, leaving a clean line in the middle of the dirt. She tried to keep herself composed as she focused with an angry look painted on her face.

"I'm sorry," Ethel said, calming down for a moment. "It

just hurts to remember. To have a childhood as I had with parents so cold makes one very sad...very sad and angry!" She pulled her hands down to reveal her suddenly ghoulish face. Ethel's eyes were sunken and black behind her crooked glasses. Her teeth turned into a rotten brown. The wrinkles on her skin were deeper. "Don't you understand!?"

Dianne and Megan leaned back in their chairs as Ethel got up from the edge of the bed. The old woman grew taller than before, towering over the sisters as if they had returned to the size of small children.

"I often think about what I'd do to them if I had the strength back then. Maybe I wouldn't let that man put his hands on me or let my mother turn the other cheek!" Ethel's face contorted; the pitch of her voice shifted. For a split second, a man's face sat behind her glasses before returning to her twisted, grandmotherly appearance. Something possessed her, crawling beneath her skin, taking control of her tongue. "Why wouldn't they hold me? Why wouldn't they love me? What did I do wrong!?"

At that moment, Dianne understood. It clicked. Without warning, the stars and planets aligned. The universe created a path to revelation. Love. Positivity. The only way to fight off the darkness, the powers of evil, the negative forces of the world. Everything came together in such a strong epiphany that Dianne shot up from her chair, stared right into Ethel's morphing eyes, and said, "I love you."

Ethel took a step back. Her frightening eyes shifted back to normal for a moment. Her ghoulish face remained, but the spirit fell silent.

"I love you, Grandma," Dianne said with a trembling voice. "Even though we've been away from you for so long, I still love you."

Ethel shuddered in surprise. The wrinkles on her face began to rise.

Had it really been this easy all along? Was Ethel Willis' spirit merely looking for the love of the grandchildren she'd never met? As Michelle said during the séance at the Ashford House, sometimes all it takes for an entity to pass on from its plane of existence is a simple message, an acknowledgment of love, or a spoken yearning. But instead of the dead needing to tell the living, the living needed to tell the dead.

Ethel Willis seemed like more than just a traditional ghost. She had rage, a shape-shifting anger that appeared more demonic than a struggling, lost soul. However, the truth was, beneath the anguish and outbursts, was a fragile being. Although she shouted like a monster and snarled like a beast, the core of Ethel was a frightened little girl. When you peeled the layers back and chipped away at the rage, all that was left was a sadness that Ethel carried her entire life, a weight so heavy that she had to mirror her father's emotions to help carry the load.

But the load was lifting now. Ethel turned back into herself, her *true* self.

"I love you, too," Megan said through her tears. She also stood up from her seat. "I'm sorry they hurt you so much, but no one's gonna hurt you now. We're not here to cause you any harm."

A cry escaped from Ethel's throat as her body transformed, shifting back to her appearance from before. Her darkened eyes began to brighten.

"We love you, and we've missed you," Dianne said.

"We've always wanted to meet you," Megan added. "We've always wanted to come visit our grandma. We don't know why our mother has deprived us of you. There's no one else we've wanted to see more than you. After all these years."

"Oh, my grandchildren," Ethel cried. She stood at the edge of the bed, shrinking down to her normal, shorter height. She looked like she was about to fall backward at any moment. "My only granddaughters. How I've longed to see you. Please." Ethel extended her fragile little arms outward. "Come give your grandmother a hug."

Then, without hesitation, without even a second thought from either of the sisters, Dianne and Megan approached the ghost of their grandmother, held out their arms, and wrapped themselves around one another in a tight embrace.

Chapter 17

The Escape

As the sisters held their grandmother close, Ethel let out one final cry before her soul escaped from her body. For a brief moment in time, she was no longer old, no longer a grandmother. She was a little girl with dark hair, crying out, weeping with tears of relief. Joy even. The sights and sounds merged until Ethel Willis' elderly form returned. The top half of her head exploded into a cloud of dust. Dianne and Megan didn't let go as the rest of her began to crumble and burst, turning Ethel's entire body into one thick pillar of dark particles that rose to the ceiling.

The room spun, and the late evening sun outside began to blink and fade. The floor trembled, sending Dianne and Megan down as lightning bolt cracks formed across the white walls in loud crackles and snaps. All the clean paint peeled away, bringing back the rotten, trashed aesthetic that the sisters knew long before they turned on the generators in the basement.

Dianne and Megan rolled into each other and embraced

on the floor, keeping their eyes shut tight as Room 222 fell apart.

The door cracked in half. The toilet exploded into white shards, sending porcelain everywhere. The dresser was destroyed along with the bed and tables. Everything erupted into dust as the entire foundation of Wing A shook.

Dianne was sure this was it, the big one. After all this time, they were destined to die after crushing the spirit of their grandmother. Their souls would be trapped inside Shaded Grove forever despite doing what Dianne thought was the right thing, giving in to what the spirit wanted: to be held, to be loved.

The wall with the window fell outward, crushing the nearby barbed wire fence with a heavy thud. Then, as Room 222 continued to crumble and spit fountains of dust onto the sisters, the floor gave way, this time creating a diagonal, sliding effect that sent Dianne and Megan rolling down the crumbling linoleum and out the fallen wall to the outside world.

Clouds of dust followed the sisters as they slid down the rubble. Tiny pieces of concrete and brick cut at their skin and sliced their faces. Dianne's temple wound reopened, bringing out hot, fresh blood that trickled down her cheek. Megan flipped sideways, breaking whatever was left of the bone in her right arm.

The fall was both fast and slow at the same time—both tall and short. The world seemed to pulsate and flash between dimensions, showing the sisters the light of the sun and the hue of the moon until their bodies stopped at the end of the fallen wall, where the broken bricks spilled before the grass. None of the barbed wire stuck out from the debris.

Dianne and Megan coughed and spat as they writhed

on the remains. Dianne swiped blood out of her eyes, feeling her hand slide over the fresh red that painted her head. She also noticed her nose was bleeding. Dianne sniffed hard but got a nostril full of dust in the mix, making her spit up dark red phlegm into the rubble.

Megan got onto her knees as she clutched her broken arm. Her neck was covered in tiny red scratches. Some bled down onto the collar of her shirt beneath her dirt and dust-covered jacket. She looked like she had spent her whole life living in the dirtiest, most forgotten attic in the world. They both did.

"Are you all right?" Megan asked.

Dianne spat up more sickly phlegm before she turned to face her sister. "I'm d-dying." She dry-heaved. "I can't...I can't breathe right."

Megan got to her feet and carefully traversed the rubble to help her sister up from the bloody mess she knelt in. She swiped Dianne's filthy black hair from her face since the strands were sticking to the blood on her cheeks. Megan's hands weren't so clean, but Dianne was in too much misery to care. With the gunk covering her face, the reds, and ashy darks of the dust, Dianne looked like a dirty newborn baby.

"You're gonna be okay, Dianne. We made it out," Megan said. "We're outside."

Sunlight began to penetrate the purple dawn sky behind the sisters. A glow came from across the treetops. It was a cool, chilled morning. No rain fell.

Just then, a loud crash came from above. The sisters looked up and saw the entire building of Wing A implode on itself. A giant mushroom cloud of dust billowed up into the sky. Just beyond, Dianne and Megan made out the other building following the same fate. Explosions of rubble and ash combined to form a nuclear-sized particle beast in the air—a monster made from the remnants of Shaded Grove Mental Hospital.

And it was coming right for them, creeping with a ghostly float.

Dianne didn't have time to see for sure, but she was sure there were faces in the cloud. Hands reaching out. Silent screams in the dust. The faces melded together, some looking like Todd the security guard, others looking like Gerald Swaggart, and the other patients. The lost souls of a time so hurtful and cruel.

With what must've been the last shot of adrenaline her body could produce, Megan pulled Dianne up from the ground and moved her off the crumbled wall, into the grass before the sea of trees ahead.

"We have to go, c'mon. This is our last chance," Megan said. She put Dianne's arm over her shoulder and walked her like she was a wounded soldier. Despite Megan's arm being cracked in two and tears flowing from her eyes, she just winced through the pain and pressed forward.

Dianne coughed and spat blood to her side so as not to hit her sister with it. The phlegm landed on a small bush. "Are we really out? Is it really...over?"

"Almost," Megan said. "Just stay with me."

Dianne spat again. "Oh, God, there's blood everywhere!"

"Don't worry about it. You're going to be okay. I promise."

Megan glanced behind her. The cloud kept its pace, wrapping its murky fingers around the trunks of the trees, following the sisters as they limped along the moist morning forest. But the sisters moved faster than the dust. Even in their weakness, they made the gap bigger between them and the dark cloud.

"I'm sorry," Dianne cried. "I'm sorry I did this to us."

"Shh. Stop that. You didn't do anything. None of this is your fault," Megan said. "Just keep moving." She lifted Dianne off the ground as they walked away from Shaded Grove. Dianne's sneakers grazed the grass below. She kicked and moved through the woods as best as she could, but Megan was doing most of the heavy lifting. Broken arm and all.

With the morning light guiding them, the sisters maneuvered through the trees, taking their time when they came across upturned roots or bundled shrubbery. They couldn't afford to stop completely, but they had to be sure they wouldn't trip and break a leg. If that were to happen, there would be no telling what the cloud of dust would do or where it would take them.

"Hey, I see a guardrail up there," Megan said as she eyed the familiar sight of roadside metal, the kind you'd find before an embankment or a sharp turn. "Do you think you can walk a little more? We just have to make it up this hill."

Dianne choked out, "Okay." The blood from her nosebleed was all over the inside and outside of her mouth. Every swallow brought a metallic taste.

Megan got behind her sister, placing her hands on her back as the earth began to curve upward. A shot of pain shot through Megan's arm like electricity. She let out a groan but didn't stop herself from walking up the embankment, pushing Dianne with every step.

"C-car," Dianne muttered.

"What?" Megan said. She turned back and saw the cloud of dust had stopped at the very bottom of the embankment. It rested against the ground, flattening into the dirt and leaves as dense fog hung in the woods. A pale white.

Extra pale. Not dark and dusty like the clouds that came from the ruined hospital.

"Car," Dianne said more clearly. "I see a car!"

Faint lights whizzed by just up ahead. The sound of a country radio station faded in and out. The scent of wet asphalt and soft dirt floated in the chilly air.

"Let's hope that wasn't the last one," Megan said as she gave her sister one final push to get her to the top of the embankment.

Dianne threw her legs over the guardrail and sat with her body facing the road. She coughed and heaved with her hands resting on her knees. Megan came around, too. She unzipped her leather jacket and flipped it inside out. It was dusty inside as well but cleaner than the outside of it. She used what parts of the leather she could to wipe the blood from her younger sister's face.

"Where was this rail when we needed it before," Megan said. "Just our luck, huh?"

Dianne swayed dizzily.

"You're all right. It looks worse than it really is," Megan said. "It's just smeared all over, is all. You're gonna live. Try to take deep breaths."

Dianne did her best to compose herself. The sight of blood on her hands was not helping, especially not the blood she saw in her spit.

"Hey, think about it like this. You'll get some time off school," Megan said.

Dianne smiled a red smile, but she was in pain. A lot of it. Megan, too. The sisters were going to be scarred for life after this. Not just on a physical level but spiritually as well. Their bodies and minds would never be the same again.

The only sounds in the chilled air were hidden birds chirping and the heavy beating hearts of Dianne and

Megan. It was a calm and cool morning despite the loud crashing of the mental hospital moments ago. There wasn't even an echo of the destruction across the sky—no signs of the floating cloud of dust. Only fog and morning dew remained.

After several minutes of Dianne and Megan trying to clean themselves up, a station wagon came around the curve in the oncoming lane, bringing a pair of orange headlights through the dawn, illuminating the sisters in a spotlight.

Megan got up from the guardrail and waved the driver down with her good hand. She jumped and shouted, "Hey! Hey! Please, help us! Hey!"

The station wagon pulled off to the side of the road not long after Megan started her cries for help.

"Thank Jesus they're stopping," Megan said, out of breath. She turned to Dianne and helped her off the guardrail. Dianne continued to sniff until she pinched her nose to stop the dripping blood.

The sisters quickly crossed the road toward the parked car as a man popped out of the driver's side door. He was big and round with a shaved head and long goatee that covered his neck.

"Holy shit," the man said as he came closer to the sisters. His eyes were wide with fright. "What happened to you two?"

"Our car flipped," Megan said. Despite her pain and misery, she was articulate. "We slid off the road last night in the rain and got lost in the mental hospital."

Megan went to continue and ask to use the man's cell phone, but the man interjected as the sight of the girls made him get right to the point.

"Sit down in the back of my car. I'll call 911 right now," he said. He patted his pockets until he leaned back into the station wagon to retrieve a flip phone. With shaking hands, he dialed emergency services and told the operator his name was Ben Mullins and to send an ambulance immediately. He began rattling off road names.

"Thank you so much," Megan said. "C'mon, Dianne, over here."

The sisters went to the side of the station wagon not facing the road. Megan opened the back passenger door and sat Dianne inside. The car smelled musty, like stale cigarettes and aged leather.

"Are you doing okay?" Megan asked.

Through her bleeding and fear, Dianne nodded.

Ben stayed on the call, explaining the situation as he went to the back of the car and opened the trunk door. He rummaged around until he pulled a folded blanket out. "I'm going to keep them in my car. They're moving and talking. The one is banged up pretty bad and bleeding from her face." With his rural accent, every syllable held emphasis, and each sound was exaggerated.

Ben came around and knelt before the sisters. He handed the blanket to Megan, who unfolded it with careful hands and wrapped it around Dianne. The blanket was blue and white with various crumbs and pieces of lint sticking to it. Much like the car, it stunk of smoke. The aroma reminded Dianne of her Uncle Tommy again.

"Thanks," Dianne muttered. She was afraid if she spoke too much, she'd spit blood all over Ben's blanket.

"They said they got lost last night after the crash, somewhere by the old hospital in the woods," Ben said into the phone. He spoke in frantic bursts. "Yeah, they're right here with me. Okay, okay." Ben lowered the phone from his ear. "Is it just the two of you? Was anyone else with you in the car?"

Neither of the sisters could even try to begin to explain the situation of last night's encounter with Ethel Willis, so they just glanced at each other until Megan said, "No, just us. Our car was completely smashed, and we lost our phones."

"Okay, yeah, no, there were no other people in the car, just the two girls," Ben said, lifting the phone back up to his ear. "Okay, thank you. I'm gonna stay right here with them."

Dianne sniffed again. Blood left a stained red ring around her mouth.

"Use this for your face," Ben said, pointing to the blanket. "I'm sorry I don't have anything better for you, but you can bleed all over that if you need, sweetheart. It's an old thing."

"The hospital blew up," Dianne said.

"What's that?" Ben said. He lowered the phone to his shoulder.

"That abandoned hospital," Megan said. "We don't know what happened, but all the buildings fell apart. That's why we're covered in all this. The whole place exploded."

Ben looked confused. "The nearest hospital is about twenty-something miles from here."

"Mental...," Dianne said. "The mental hospital. We found it after the crash. We almost died just from the dust."

Ben's bewilderment never left his face. The big man must've thought the sisters were talking crazy from all their injuries. "There's no mental hospital around here, hasn't been for a little while. You probably got yourselves lost by the old site."

"What? Not far from here, there's a whole complex. That's where we just came from," Megan said.

Another car came around the curve but didn't stop.

Ben shook his head. "I'm sorry, that place was torn

down a while back. Maybe ten years ago. You two might've gotten yourselves worked up out there, but don't worry, the ambulance will be here soon. Just try to be calm and relax yourselves."

Dianne and Megan were too broken down to react to Ben's claim that Shaded Grove Mental Hospital hadn't stood for years. There would be plenty of time for the two of them to get their facts straight once they received the proper medical treatment. There was no sense starting a back and forth with Ben, even though the sisters were covered in the dust that came from the crumbled Wing A and the various patients they encountered. How could Ben explain that?

The sisters looked at each other with their sunken eyes and tired souls. Although they were out of the hospital and away from Ethel Willis, their sense of victory hadn't set in yet. Only when they were away from the town of Shaded Grove and back into the care of their mother would they feel as though they'd made it out alive. All that they hoped for now was to be taken to a hospital that wasn't abandoned, torn down, or thrown into another dimension.

As a morning bird flew overhead and chirped into the fog, the sound of sirens came echoing from the distance.

Chapter 18

The Next Few Days

Megan's right arm was as broken as broken could be. It had suffered so much trauma from the car crash and the events that played out in the mental hospital that nuts and bolts had to hold the pieces of bone back together with the help of tiny plates, thin slices of metal that looked so out of place on the X-ray pictures.

Megan got twenty-six stitches when it was all said and done. She would have to keep her arm stabilized for a few months in a cast and sling. No more waiting tables for a while, just a lot of resting and Extra Strength Tylenol.

But Megan's arm wasn't the only part of her body that suffered injuries. After spending so much time breathing in dust and filthy fumes from Shaded Grove Mental Hospital, or wherever the doctors and nurses believed the sisters were that night, Megan's lungs had a considerable amount of damage. In-between her downing pain meds, Megan had to use an inhaler to administer a bitter-tasting chemical spray that would help clean the airways of the grime she ingested. Dianne, too, had an inhaler prescribed to her.

Although Dianne didn't break any bones herself, she had to get a few stitches on her left temple. She had to take antibiotics to fight off the potentially infected area since it was cut open on such a jagged, dirty piece of brick. The doctor said she was lucky it didn't get her eye. The way it had sliced her could've blinded her left eye if it would've carved over a few more centimeters.

Yes, the Willis sisters were pretty banged up, but they were lucky enough to be driven to Golden Creek Medical Center, which was, as Ben stated, over twenty miles away. It was the same hospital Megan found on her GPS on the night they almost ran over Ethel Willis. She was going to drive her grandmother there until Ethel started losing her mind.

Much like Shaded Grove, Golden Creek was a tucked-away town off the highway, kind of run-down, kind of outdated. It took a minute for Deborah, the girls' mother, to find the hospital considering it was a bit of a hike to get there. She planned on driving out to Shaded Grove after her girls didn't pick up their phones from the night before. It always drove Deborah nuts when she couldn't reach either of her daughters, so as the night grew later and later, Deborah got desperate.

The cops were called. Neighbors were woken up. Deborah even had to sign on to Facebook to contact Gage, Megan's boyfriend, who was also unable to get in touch with the sisters. Deborah and Gage kept in touch through the night and coordinated a drive to Shaded Grove together when Deborah received a call from the Golden Creek Medical Center with Megan's shaky voice coming from the other end. Deborah was so relieved and anxious that she left the house without letting Gage know they were safe. She was so eager to get to her children that she forgot to inform anyone of her departure.

Deborah spent the next few days with her daughters until they were well enough to be discharged. She had to stay in a cheap hotel during the nights in Golden Creek, but she was right by the hospital so that she could visit Dianne and Megan throughout the days. With their mother there with them, the Willis sisters recovered a whole lot faster. Deborah's presence brought positive, healing energy, the kind only a mother could bring in a time of such pain and fear.

Of course, there was no easy way of getting into the whole situation with their mother. Dianne and Megan wanted to tell their tale of the ghost tour, E. W, finding the old woman in the street, and the horrific crash that led them to Shaded Grove Mental Hospital that apparently no longer existed, but much like with Ben Mullins, and the nurses and doctors, Deborah dismissed all as head trauma and shock. She was in no headspace herself to discuss the infamous Ethel Willis. Deborah said she would only get into that later once everyone was back home and safe, away from the distant small towns and supernatural adventures. Although Deborah was sure to tell Dianne, "No more ghost tours, at least not out of town ones. Keep your birthday trips local."

Gage Johnson arrived the night before the sisters were discharged. Not only was it great for Megan to see him with his messy brown hair and tattoos that crawled up his arms, but it was also wonderful to have someone actually listen to her and Dianne's experience with an open mind. Gage wasn't quick to dismiss everything, and he seemed to believe everything the sisters told him. Unlike the adults, Gage was willing to go along with the tales of the paranormal. Even if he didn't necessarily believe in all the ghostly and ghoulish things, he was there for the girls.

During the last night in the hospital, Megan stayed up with Gage as late as visitors were allowed and researched the history of Shaded Grove Mental Hospital. If it was true that the hospital was torn down years ago, Megan had to know. Even though she found herself believing in ghosts now, finding out that the entire mental hospital itself was a ghost would be even crazier and more life changing. Deborah, on the other hand, wasn't interested in any of it. At least not for the moment.

Despite being only able to use her left hand, it didn't take long for Megan to come across some news articles and websites surrounding the old hospital and its controversial history. There were a handful of conflicting reports, however, the timeline of Shaded Grove's operation and the incompetency of its founders seemed to be consistent throughout the articles.

Originally built in 1949, and opened in 1951, Shaded Grove Mental Hospital was planned to be Central Pennsylvania's premier mental health institution, capable of taking in patients on any point on the spectrum from all over the state. People would find that the hospital was so revolutionary in turning around patients that more hospitals would be put up statewide. That was the dream of its founders, Dr. Winston Phelps, a psychologist, and Michael Gardner III, a businessman from Philadelphia. According to the research, the two men were determined to create their own private mental health business without the constraints of the Commonwealth of Pennsylvania.

At the time, Phelps and Gardner sold themselves as having the blueprints for the latest and greatest psychological treatment facility inside and out, from the most effective forms of therapy to the best, most suitable living spaces for patients that would sit on either side of the main campus. There would be state-of-the-art security and top-tier record keeping. With the combination of Dr. Phelps' smarts and Mr. Gardner's business expertise, it would seem to any layperson that there would be no problem implementing their bulletproof plan. However, due to the Commonwealth's ruling on establishing hospital properties, the duo had to negotiate a deal to build on lands not within 100 miles of any state hospital, leaving Phelps and Gardner to place their facility in the small town of Shaded Grove.

The locals of Shaded Grove resisted the new hospital as there was a strong stigma against the mentally ill, especially at the time and place. With little understanding of psychological illnesses, the residents of Shaded Grove were frightened of the new hospital being built in their backyard. There were fears of patients escaping and children being abducted. The anxiety didn't matter, though, as Phelps and Gardner went ahead with their plan. Having the money for the ambitious project made the locals' grievances irrelevant, at least at first.

Time went on, and Shaded Grove Mental Hospital was built. Patients started to be admitted from nearby counties. Therapies took place. Doctors prescribed medications. Schedules were implemented. Security guards did their jobs. There were no escapes, no abductions of the local children. The only controversies that went on were behind closed doors, including the financial tensions between the business partners and a major sewage flood that ruined the interior of the patients' wings.

By the late fifties and early sixties, the hospital had run out of money. Shaded Grove wasn't turning around enough new patients due to the cost of being kept in the facility, and the patients who were admitted either weren't getting any better or were dying from the harmful fever treatments and dangerous electro-shock therapies, which were far from being properly regulated. The still-experimental remedies and the plummeting profits caused Phelps and Gardner's dream of building a mental health empire to fall before their very eyes.

If that weren't enough, angered families were writing to Phelps and Gardner and the local papers, demanding compensation for the mistreatment of their family and friends who were admitted. This led to multiple lawsuits being settled out of court, depleting whatever funds they had left and bringing Shaded Grove Mental Hospital to an early end.

Bankruptcy coupled with a growing snowball of bad PR, the mental hospital shut its doors in 1961, not to be opened again until a brief period from 2009 to 2011 after the state purchased the property and attempted to resume operations after decades of abandonment and decay. However, the hospital's foundation was too unstable, and the attempts to update the technology in the buildings failed to create a safe enough environment for the few patients who were admitted in the two years they reopened. Shaded Grove Mental Hospital was closed again, this time for good, as the entire facility was demolished in 2012, leaving behind nothing but a massive patch of rubble to be overgrown with weeds and eventually merging with the surrounding woods.

The state still owns the land and may rebuild another structure on the property in the future, but as of today, there are no plans for another mental institution to be placed in the small Pennsylvania town of Shaded Grove.

Reading through it all and seeing the photos of the

hospital being destroyed by bulldozers made Megan's stomach drop and roll. She couldn't believe that it had been years since the old place stood, and yet she and Dianne spent an entire night inside, seeing the rooms, walking the hallways, finding the ancient equipment, and, above all, interacting with the lost souls of the patients. They were ghosts, ghosts within the biggest ghost of all.

Chapter 19

The End of a Long Nightmare

Afternoon sunlight streamed into Dianne's room, where posters of Paramore and Harry Styles and small shelves of crystals stared back at one another. Dianne sat up in her bed as Megan sat at the desk, using Dianne's laptop to find more photos and stories of Shaded Grove.

November was moving along steadily, Dianne had just celebrated her sixteenth birthday, and soon it would be Thanksgiving. December. Winter break. Christmas. Snowfall. More time to heal and reflect.

The sisters had spent all their time together since they came home from the hospital, and they showed no signs of wanting that to change. They were closer than ever before. Megan even told Dianne that she'd wait for her to turn eighteen so that they could get matching tattoos based on their experience, a time they'd never forget.

"You know, I've been thinking," Dianne said. Her stitches were clean and healing nicely on the side of her face. "All the people in the hospital, do you think they've all moved on?"

Megan shrugged with her back facing Dianne. "Hard to say."

"Because I know there were more patients in Wing B, and we never went inside there."

Megan didn't reply. She was focused on the computer.

"Do you think we'll have to go back someday?" Dianne asked.

"No way." Megan blew air from her nose. "We're never going back to that place ever again. There's no hospital to even go back to anyway. Let someone else free the other ghosts. We did our job."

Dianne looked over to the window. "I hope so."

Neither of the sisters had any paranormal experiences since they escaped from Shaded Grove. No old women in the streets. No spirits on their shoulders. Not even nightmares plagued their sleep. Maybe they were safe since they were away from the town, or maybe they fulfilled their duty after all, and their souls were freed from the chains of Ethel Willis.

The bedroom door squeaked open, and Deborah Willis stepped inside. She looked so much like her daughters with her jet-black hair, pale skin, and thin figure. In a few years, the three of them would all look like sisters.

"How are you girls feeling?" Deborah asked. She looked at what Megan had pulled up on the laptop and sighed. "Still obsessed with that place?"

"How can we not be?" Megan said. "Wouldn't it be on your mind twenty-four seven if you survived through an abandoned mental hospital?"

Deborah took a deep breath. "Fair enough." She went to the end table and started cleaning up the bowl of soup and leftover crust from Dianne's dinner.

"Thanks," Dianne said.

Deborah took the dishes out into the kitchen and placed them in the sink. She returned to the bedroom, where she stood silent for a moment, staring at the window and what was left of the late sun.

"How are *you* feeling?" Megan asked. "Are you holding up okay?"

"Yes, I'm okay," Deborah said before she rubbed her head. Her face drooped tiredly. "I just don't know how to get into all this, but I guess I have to try. I promised you both I would explain everything once I got some of my bearings back."

"You mean about Grandma?" Dianne asked.

Deborah nodded. "Yes, about Grandma." She sighed again. "You know, it's so bizarre to me that after all these years of trying to keep you two safe and away from her, you two go and have this wild psychic séance stuff happen. The mental hospital and everything. I mean..." Deborah covered her eyes for a second. "I didn't want you girls going to Shaded Grove at all even though I don't believe in all that stuff you're into, but I figured I'd sound crazy trying to explain everything to you."

Dianne and Megan looked at each other and then back at their mother.

"Well, now is a good time as ever," Megan said.

"All right, well, to put it nicely, your grandmother was a real piece of work."

"You're telling us," Megan said under her breath.

"Yeah, that's why I was so disturbed when you told me you saw her, her ghost, or whatever it was," Deborah said. "I knew you two weren't lying when you described her mood changes, that sudden rage she has. I've had to deal with that my entire life. That's why I've kept you away and told you she died a long time ago, before you were born, Dianne. But

I guess that didn't quite work, did it? She found her way to you through that medium, that little ghost tour you went on."

"So, really, it's Dianne's fault this all happened," Megan said.

"Shut up," Dianne said.

"Oh, c'mon, I'm just messing around."

"Let Mom finish."

Deborah shrugged and said, "There's not really much to say. My mother had me when she was older. My father, who *did* die not long before you two were born, was a good man and father, but he wasn't educated or emotionally intelligent enough to handle my mother. She had a lot of mental issues, and it weighed on our family, your uncle especially. I think he has more coping issues than I do, but we're still here, we're still standing. When it comes to your grandfather, my dad, his old heart just couldn't take it anymore. His heavy smoking didn't help either, but when you're under constant stress, constantly having to be on edge for whatever my mom was going to do, it takes a real toll on your body."

"What exactly was Grandma's problem?" Megan asked.

"Well, it stems from her childhood. I don't think she grew up in a happy home, and whatever her abusive parents did to her, she did to us. As strange as it sounds, my mother screamed and spanked us more than you'd think a father would. My dad never laid a finger on me. I think he was so scared of Mom that he took a backseat when times got rough, which was always unpredictable." Deborah looked down to the carpeted floor. Her eyes welled a bit. "And that was the scariest thing about her. She would seem fine one moment and then completely out of her mind the next. We didn't even do anything to set her off, but something would switch on in her mind, and she'd be crying, screaming, and throwing things across the room. She would threaten us and become this whole other person."

Dianne knew exactly what their mother was talking about. She and Megan had front row seats to their grandmother's mood swings. They heard the shouts; they saw the monstrous shift in her old face.

"But time goes on, and you learn to tolerate people like that. At least to the best of your mental ability. It wasn't easy, especially when you're watching your own mother turn into a raging lunatic, but you almost become numb to it, you know what I mean? You come to this strange acceptance of your mother. She may not be right in the head, but you still love her somewhere deep down in your heart, even if you feel like you hate her guts, and you want to do whatever you can to make the days go a little easier. I don't know. I guess I just tried to push through all the pain she put on us. Now your uncle, on the other hand, would run away from home and do whatever he could to be away from her. There were times he wouldn't even call to check in. I think that also broke my dad's heart. Mom was so out of control that Tommy was afraid to even call to talk to him because he thought Mom would get on the phone and go into a manic phase or something like that. I can only imagine when my parents were alone what your grandmother must've said and done to your grandfather."

"Wow. Why didn't Grandpa just leave her?" Megan asked.

Deborah sighed. "You just didn't do that back in the day. It was frowned upon, I guess, but someone still would've had to look after her. She wouldn't have just calmed down after being left alone because when your grandfather passed, things got worse. Despite her older age, she would still get so fired up, so angry at things that we didn't know how else to help her. Uncle Tommy didn't want anything to do with her, and I was soon-to-be pregnant with you, Megan, at the time. Your father was still on the scene, of course. That made it a little easier for me to make the decision to put her in a mental institution. I at least had him to fall back on while I tried to get your grandmother situated somewhere, although we didn't have much money to have her admitted in most places. Someone had to pay for her care, and we sure as hell didn't want her in a regular nursing home. She needed serious psychological help."

"So, you shipped her out to Shaded Grove," Megan said.

Deborah shook her head and wiped a tear from her eye. Dianne got up and handed her mother a tissue. Deborah dabbed her cheek with it. "Not at first. She was in the state hospital for a few years. We had her in Harrisburg. Her insurance covered half of it after your grandfather passed. They put her on pills, sedated her, and all that. She honestly seemed a little better at first, but pretty soon, she was right back to having violent outbursts, attacking the staff, making threats to other patients. My God, I mean, it was like this rage in her went beyond all the medications and therapies."

"Jeez," Dianne said. "So *that's* why you didn't want us near her?"

Another tear spilled down Deborah's cheek. "Right, I was raising Megan, and then you were born, Dianne. I had my hands full. Your father and I were getting into our own bullshit, our own disagreements. Your grandmother was the *last* person who needed to be involved in your lives, so I kept you two hidden away from her. I mean, I was angry with her. I was angry with your father. I felt myself starting to get that rage, that same explosiveness my mother had, and I did not want to become like her. I swore when I was young that I wasn't going to turn into the mother she was to me and my brother, or the wife she was to my father." She swiped away more tears. "I didn't even know if I could ever have children myself because I was so afraid of having her genetics or passing them on. But life just happens, you know? You try to move on, you try to make the best of things, do what's right."

Dianne and Megan got emotional themselves as they listened to their mother's story. They felt for their mother and loved her deeply. Deborah had done the best she could, and if it weren't for their time in Shaded Grove and hearing the story now, Dianne and Megan would have never guessed their mom came from such hostility.

"Your grandmother wanted to meet the two of you," Deborah said. "I would tell her that children weren't allowed in the mental hospital and that maybe when she got better, she could have a day outside to meet you in the park. I would make up all these lies which would eventually make her angrier, so I started bringing in pictures of the two of you to try to give her something, anything to make her calm down. And they worked for a little while. But time went on, and she was just getting worse and worse. She was losing all this weight."

"I would visit her, and she'd scream that she hated me and that I was abandoning her and keeping her grand-daughters away from her. That I was cruel. The hospital was getting concerned, and soon the insurance money was dwindling, and your father and I's marriage was ending. I was trying to balance everything out. I felt like I was in the middle of a tug-of-war, and I was being pulled in every direction. The divorce came. All these fees came with that, especially when I asked the lawyer to get your last name changed back to Willis. I was all over the place, trying to fix all I thought was broken."

Deborah covered her face again, failing to stop herself from breaking down and sobbing like a baby. Dianne and Megan wept. Tears streamed down their cheeks.

"And then we had to transfer her to Shaded Grove," Deborah said, talking through her tears. "That was the only place we could afford to put her. As you know, with all that research you're doing on the internet there, they opened the place back up for a little bit. It was cheaper. I was in-between jobs, and your father had enough saved so that we could put her in there and see how she did for a few months, but she passed away not long after she was admitted. I think the move there was too much for her mental state, and it pushed her over the edge. I visited her there as much as I physically could, but her body just gave out, and she died one morning. She never woke up. They said she had a stroke in her sleep." Deborah sobbed. "And even though she caused such pain, I still felt guilty. I felt like I had done something wrong, like I didn't work hard enough to take care of my mother and left her all alone to die in some run-down hospital in a faraway place where she didn't know where she was."

There was a pause, and the only sound in the room came from the sniffling sobs of the three Willis women. Dianne got up from the bed and embraced her mother. Megan joined in. The three of them cried in each other's arms as the overwhelming weight of it all fell on them.

"You didn't do anything wrong, Mom," Dianne said as she wept into her mother's shoulder. "You did all that you could. You did the right thing."

"I just didn't want you to see her," Deborah cried. "I

didn't want you two to be scared of her like I was. She could've done something to you, had an outburst."

"We're sorry she was so hurtful to you," Megan said.

Deborah pulled back from the hug. She wiped her face and sniffed. "I hope you know how much I love you two and that I'd never want you to go through anything like that, even if it's because of me. I'd rather die than put you through that."

The sisters shook their heads.

"We love you," Megan said. "You're a great mom. You've always been a great mom."

Dianne nodded in agreement, unable to speak in her emotional state.

"And you've been great daughters. I'm so proud of you both, and I'm so happy you're home safe with me," Deborah said. "Just promise me no more ghost stuff, okay?"

They laughed and hugged again, letting the rest of their tears fall.

"I mean, my God," Deborah said, trying to blink out the eyelashes caught in her red eyes. "I just never thought something like this would happen. It doesn't seem real. Making contact, having that medium lady say her initials to you. You two could've been killed in that crash, for Christ's sake. But you know what, in some twisted, crazy way, I guess my mother got her wish, after all. She got to meet her granddaughters."

"So, you believe us?" Dianne said.

Deborah looked down and nodded. "I believe you. I'm not sure how or why it had to be this way, and it still hasn't really hit me yet, but yes, I believe you. Just like you always talk about, Dianne, it all manifested. The powers of the universe. Energies and all that. I guess you're right about it all. I just wish it didn't have to flip your car and almost get you two killed."

"Yeah, I don't think I'm gonna go on any more tours for a while," Dianne said. "Now that I know what they're capable of."

"I think that's a good idea. And if you want my honest opinion, I wouldn't be looking up any more stuff about Shaded Grove. If you think your grandmother's at peace, there's no sense harping on it too much longer. I wouldn't want her to come back and haunt you. Believe me, I've been haunted enough," Deborah said. She took a deep breath and fanned her face with her hands. "Well, now I'm overheated. I'm sorry to get all into that, but you can see why I wasn't itching to get into everything while you two were in the hospital. But maybe I still said all that too soon. Maybe tonight wasn't the right time."

"No, Mom, you're okay. We're glad you told us. It gives us closure," Megan said, using her left hand to wipe her nose. "I'm sorry you had to relive the trauma."

Deborah smiled and said, "Oh, honey, don't worry about me. I'll be all right. I'm not the one with a broken arm or a set of stitches. Now you two need your rest. If we stay up all night talking about old Ethel Willis, her damn ghost is going to show up in *my* life, and I have work in the morning."

"Okay. No more ghost stuff," Dianne said. "Meg won't look up any more stories online either."

"Right," Megan said. "We won't bring it up unless you do, Mom."

Deborah nodded. "Sounds like a plan." She hugged her daughters once more and walked back to the doorway. "Holler if you need anything tonight. Don't stay up too late. I know how you girls can get if you're together too long."

"We won't," Megan said. "Holler if you need anything from us, too."

"You got it. Love you both to bits," Deborah said before exiting Dianne's room.

"Love you, too," the sisters said in unison. They shuffled back to their spots, Dianne on the bed and Megan sitting at the desk. Megan exited out of the Wikipedia article on Shaded Grove Mental Hospital and closed the laptop.

Dianne pulled the covers up to her neck. Glancing out the window at the setting sun, she saw her mother walking out to the porch, cigarette in hand, staring out into the horizon of the fading day. "Looks like Mom is lighting one up for the occasion."

"I don't blame her," Megan said, coming to the window to get a look at her mother, who hadn't smoked in over a decade. "After all this, she deserves one. She'd probably let *us* take a puff. Don't you think?" She shot her sister a smile.

"Probably," Dianne said. "But I think we'd need something stronger than that."

"You ain't wrong, sis," Megan said. "Do you need anything? I'm gonna try to take a bath and hope I don't get my arm wet."

"I'm good, but thanks. Let me know if you need help."

Megan moved over to the door. "Yeah, treat me just like Gerald Swaggart, right?"

Dianne shook her head. "Don't think about him."

"How can I not? That was the most disgusting part of the whole night!" Megan joked.

"You're a weirdo," Dianne said as her sister left the room. She looked back to the window, watching the little tufts of smoke swirl from the top of her mother's cigarette. Her mind wandered. Gerald Swaggart. He was someone's son. He could've also been someone's father, brother, husband. Was there a living person out there who could set his soul free?

Ethel Willis. The patients. The doctors. Were they all still there, roaming the halls of the torn-down mental hospital? If so, who would be the one to free them, to help them pass on to the next life? Was it even possible, or are the spirits of the damned, the lost and forgotten, destined to stay someplace in-between for all eternity? What about the Ashford family? Where were they right now?

Dianne shut her eyes for a moment as she tried to settle herself down. Her heart still raced from her mother's emotional story. It was all overwhelming and heavy on Dianne. Too much to take in with a single thought, too frightening to understand with just one telling of it. She wondered how her mother was able to carry herself so well, considering the pain she endured as a child along with carrying the guilt of her mother's passing to this day. Dianne could see how that could crumble one's soul to pieces and leave families in ruins. Maybe that was why it didn't work out with her parents. It was all too much to balance out between them—the emotional weight.

Would that happen to Dianne if she got married in the future? Would Megan be able to start a family and keep it together? It seemed like the sisters were on a straight enough path, even if their lives were forever changed by the night they spent in Shaded Grove. It's possible that no one would ever believe their tale of how they survived through a ghostly hospital after being drawn in by their dead grandmother. Still, one thing was for certain, the Willis girls had an unbreakable bond, a relationship as hard as bedrock. Not only between the two of them but their mother as well, because if it wasn't for Deborah's strength and love, the

Willis sisters might not have made it out of Shaded Grove alive.

Megan ran water from the bathtub's faucet in the bathroom across the hall. Deborah snuffed out her cigarette on the ground and came back inside through the swinging screen door. Dianne turned away from the window as her mind continued to swirl with thoughts. She would let them come and go, passing through her mind like an infinite pipeline. But it was all right because Dianne was safe now, and even if she felt scared, her mother and sister would be there for her, just like she would be there for them. Always.

Acknowledgments

I cannot thank Laura and Matt Hughes enough for believing in this story and having it be a part of Stag Beetle Books' wonderful catalog. Working with you has been incredible and I appreciate you and the Stag Beetle Books team very much, especially Cheyenne Cooley, who helped me polish and edit Shaded Grove to be the best book it could be.

I'd like to thank my wonderful family, who has provided nothing but unconditional love and support. My mother, father, brother, Gram Good, Pap and Gram Seneca, Rachel, Caroline, William aka Squilliam, Dustin, Aunt Linda, Aunt Pam, Aunt Carol, and Uncle Jim.

I have to thank my dear friends and second family: Kelmich "Kermit" Agosto, Ashley Rosado, Damien Holmes, Natalie Miller, Autumn Marou, Karla and Jessica Dumas, Missy Brenneman, Tiffany Golobek, Ms. Vikki Williams, and Becki Hatzimichael.

Thanks to Brandon Ulp and the rest of the Ulp clan, Mike and Vicki Brown, the Signori crew, Steven Grier Williams, Jerry Roth, David Walton, and B.A. Colella.

Also thanks to Dave Gray, Gabby Irwin, Bree Antonio, Bonita Brown, Asim Pervaiz, Matt Warner, Tara Miller, Tyler Poust, Kelli Cummings, Anthony Anderson, Wes Slaugh, Krishna Adhikari, Duka Dhakal, Ari Nodjigoto, Christina Seifert, Julia Sheffer, Jill Lutz, Raeshell Evans, Kyra Gadsden, Liz Hill, Kada Louis, Linda Lee, Nick

Byzek, Jeremy Kitner, Kirk Bloom, Abbie Smith, Kim Wrightstone, Mandi Shoop, Mike Davis, Shawn Vice, Stacey Kelley, Laura Dundorf, Louis Williams, Francois Bakafwa Kayembe, Bouchria El Amri, Derek Davis, Brandon Link, Candice Booker, Argentina Adler, Deacon Derstler, Richard Baskeyfield, Chuck Zito, Anthony "Kid" Mercurio, Reinaldo Rosario, Ashley Eichelberger, Tina Brosius, Hom Phuyel, Nadine Lewandowski, Maley Lysle, Brittany McDaniel, and everyone at ThredUp who went out of their way to help me during my wonderful time there.

And thanks to all the good people at Dempsey who have been so patient with me.

Finally, I'd like to thank you, the reader. It's always a pleasure.

I'll see you in the next one!

About the Author

Oliver C. Seneca is a graduate of Pennsylvania State University.

His novels, When the Sky Goes Dark and Faces in a Window, were published by Sunbury Press. You can find his short fiction and poetry included in Scare Street's Night Terrors, Open Minds Quarterly, and Black Hare Press's Anthologies.

From the Publisher

Thank you so much for reading Shaded Grove!

We hope you enjoyed the journey and characters as much as we loved bringing them to you. **Please leave a review on Amazon** and Goodreads while the story is fresh in your mind. Reviews are writing fuel for authors and help their books get into the hands of other hungry readers.

If you're a big fan of speculative young adult and middle-grade fiction, we invite you to join our street team. Get copies of our books in advance, early access to covers, and other freebies!

Stag Beetle Books
www.stagbeetlebooks.com

www.ingramcontent.com/pod-product-compliance
Lightning Source LLC
Chambersburg PA
CBHW020023310726
48970CB00007B/2175